An Unforeseen Love 3

Meesha

Lock Down Publications and Ca$h
Presents
An Unforeseen Love 3
A Novel by *Meesha*

2

Lock Down Publications
Po Box 944
Stockbridge, Ga 30281

Visit our website @
www.lockdownpublications.com

Copyright 2022 by Meesha
An Unforeseen Love 3

First Edition July 2022
Printed in the United States of America

This is a work of fiction. Names, characters, places, and incidents either are products of the author's imagination or are used fictitiously. Any similarity to actual events or locales or persons, living or dead, is entirely coincidental.

Lock Down Publications
Like our page on Facebook: Lock Down Publications @
www.facebook.com/lockdownpublications.ldp
Book interior design by: **Shawn Walker**
Edited by: **Jill Alicea**

Stay Connected with Us!

Text **LOCKDOWN** to 22828 to stay up-to-date with new releases,
sneak peaks, contests and more…
Thank you.

Submission Guideline.

Submit the first three chapters of your completed manuscript to ldpsubmissions@gmail.com, subject line: Your book's title. The manuscript must be in a .doc file and sent as an attachment. Document should be in Times New Roman, double spaced and in size 12 font. Also, provide your synopsis and full contact information. If sending multiple submissions, they must each be in a separate email.

Have a story but no way to send it electronically? You can still submit to LDP/Ca$h Presents. Send in the first three chapters, written or typed, of your completed manuscript to:

LDP: Submissions Dept
Po Box 944
Stockbridge, Ga 30281

DO NOT send original manuscript. Must be a duplicate.

Provide your synopsis and a cover letter containing your full contact information.

Thanks for considering LDP and Ca$h Presents.

Meesha

Chapter 1

'Cause when a woman's fed up
No matter how you beg, no
It ain't nothing you can do about it
It's like running out of love
No matter what you say, no
And it's too late to talk about it...

"Man, if you don't turn that bullshit off!" Chade yelled over the music as he walked into Samir's mancave. "You know damn well we banned that nigga Kelz, and here you are sitting in this bitch staring at the wall, feeling sorry for yo'self. And why the fuck yo' door wasn't locked? Anybody could've come through this bitch and robbed yo' ass."

Chade's professionalism went out the door when he was around his friends and family. His Chicago street mannerism was on full display as he looked around his friend's mancave. The way Samir looked pissed his boy off to the highest point of pisstivity. It was his own fault he was in the jam he was in and Chade understood, but life doesn't stop after a break-up.

"Come on, man. Get up and unleash this funk!"

Samir had been sitting in the same spot for the past two days. The only time he moved was when he had to use the bathroom or refilled his glass. Eating and showering was the furthest thing from his mind. Since Selena packed her shit and moved out two months prior, her absence had his head fucked up. Being in the house he bought for his wife alone was something he was trying to cope with. But being without the love of his life and his baby girl was taking a toll on him mentally.

"Nigga, hello! Are you fuckin' listening?"

"My bad, bro. This shit with Selena is really getting to me. She's not fuckin' with a nigga on no level, and I don't know what to do. I fucked up, Chade. I need my family back."

Chade watched his friend sulk in his sorrows and felt bad for the situation he was in. The last thing he wanted was for his long-time friend falling headfirst into depression. Chade was tired of hearing people of color say "depression isn't real". No matter what ethnicity, depression has crippled many. Amongst black people, it was always deemed as someone looking for attention or pretending. That's not the case at all. Muthafuckas better seek help for that shit, because it can destroy a person in a matter of time.

"Well, sitting in this dark-ass basement wallowing around isn't doing you any good. I've been calling you for hours, and I'm glad I decided to come by and check on you," Chade said, looking around the room in disgust. "Get up so you can take a shower! It looks like a damn alley in here. All these damn empty alcohol bottles thrown around isn't a good look, bro. Where are the food containers? Have you been eating?"

"Man, I'm not hungry. You act like you don't drink on occasion. Don't judge me, Chade."

"Samir, you know me better than that. I would never judge you, but the shit I'm seeing right now isn't you at all. Drinking all day without eating isn't healthy and will lead you down a path that you will have trouble turning back from. That shit is only patching up the hurt you're feeling. When the buzz wears off, you gon' be right back at square one. I'm not about to stand here and act like I don't see you're on a road to destruction. Come on. Go get cleaned up. I want you to take a ride with me."

Chade pulled his friend up from the lounge chair and escorted him into the bathroom on the other side of the mancave. Once Samir closed the door, Chade went to work cleaning up the mess his friend had made. Witnessing firsthand how the separation was affecting Samir, Chade had already made up his mind to help. He just didn't know where to start.

Since Baylei entered his life, Chade was learning how to live life thinking about someone other than himself, and the shit was no walk in the park. He was used to sleeping with numerous women with no strings attached, then suddenly he was engaged to be married. Samir had been married three years, and his situation opened

8

Chade's eyes to the not-so-happy side of marriage. He was definitely taking notes on what not to do when it was time to say "I do", because Baylei wasn't going for the cheating shit.

As Chade rustled around on the other side of the door, Samir sat on the toilet with tears falling from his eyes. He never wanted his friends to see how low he'd fallen. Drinking had become a part of his daily routine. Masking the shit only when he went into work, Samir was struggling to get through the day without the liquid poison. Stepping out on Selena was something he wished he'd never done. He thought back on the day he allowed his irritation with his wife to lead him to Lavita's bed. The bathroom was hot from the steam of the shower, causing his nose to run. After blowing his nose, Selina's voice filled his mind.

"Please, don't touch me, Samir. My back hurts, my feet are swollen, and I can't eat anything without throwing it back up. This isn't the way I expected pregnancy to be!" Selena screamed as she moved out of his reach on the bed.

"Whatever I can do to ease your discomfort, I'm here for you. You're not going through this pregnancy alone, Selena," Samir said, placing his wife's feet in his lap. He started massaging the sole of her foot and she snatched it away, slightly hitting his dick in the process.

"I asked you not to touch me! You don't know what the fuck it feels like to carry all this excess weight around every fucking day! You are still physically fit while I'm getting bigger by the minute!"

"Baby, you are beautiful. I don't care how much weight you gain; my baby is the reason you look better than before with a twist. You may be uncomfortable now, but we will get you back to the shape you had once you heal. No matter what, I love you just the way you are, Selena."

Samir's words of encouragement went in one ear and out the other because Selena wasn't trying to hear anything he said. The bickering and bitching about her weight, being sick, and not wanting to be bothered went on throughout the entire pregnancy starting from her second trimester. Samir was there every step of the way, trying to make things easier, but after a while, he drifted away from the woman he loved. He stayed close to home and out of Selena's way, but she found reasons to argue at every turn.

Selena was excited when she first learned of her pregnancy, but unbeknownst to Samir, her excitement deflated after researching pregnancy deaths and miscarriages in the early stages. She was also afraid of the rapid weight gain that she was sure to endure throughout the nine months of carrying a child. The stories she read of men leaving their significant others because of their body changes was another situation that put her on edge.

As the weeks turned into months, Lavita's attention and office affection filled the void his wife no longer provided. They would talk, laugh, and joke around to pass time. Samir didn't think too much about it when Lavita would bring breakfast and have lunch packed for him every day. Samir spoke highly of his wife every chance he got while in Lavita's presence. He never wanted her to forget that he was a married man.

From eight in the morning until six in the evening, Samir and Lavita worked closely with one another, and it never went outside the walls of Wells Fargo Bank. The sexual tension was electrifying between the two, and Samir didn't attempt to put a stop to the heavy flirting they were doing after a while. One day, Lavita offered to treat him to lunch because she was too tired to prepare anything the night before. Samir didn't intend to take things to unforbidden territories, but it had been a month since Selena gave up the pussy and he needed to be in some gushy shit before he exploded. Instead of going out to eat, Samir fed Lavita his dick and fucked her every which way he could. And that was the day Lavita officially became his work wife.

Every day thereafter, at least three times a week, they were rolling around in a suite at the Sheraton hotel. Her father owned a timeshare and the room was always available for her to use whenever she wanted, and the two of them took advantage. Thirty to forty-five minutes was all it took for them to get their rocks off while on lunch with time to spare to get back to the bank. There was even a couple times Samir took Lavita across town on somewhat of a date on Saturdays so they wouldn't be seen by anyone he knew.

Samir felt bad for dipping out on his wife, but Selena was always too tired or just didn't want to go out when he suggested it. If she received a call or text from her assistant about her photography business, she would muster up the strength to do whatever was needed, but didn't put the same effort into her husband. Once Selena noticed Samir was just existing in the house, she became suspicious. She never addressed the situation until she had proof though. Selena could tell Samir was withdrawn and didn't think it had anything to do with her attitude or lack of affection. All she knew was that her husband had stopped trying to pamper her and kept his distance.

"What are you doing in there, nigga? It doesn't take that long for any man to shower!"

Chade banging on the door brought Samir out of his thoughts. Glancing up at the clock on the wall, he didn't realize he'd been in the bathroom forty minutes. The shower was running for no reason because he hadn't thought about getting in the shower the entire time he was in there.

"I'm on my way out. I was distracted. Give me five minutes!" Samir yelled.

Quickly jumping in the shower, Samir hurried up and washed his body in the lukewarm water and then hopped out. Chade wasn't going to wait too long for Samir to make his exit. Before long, he was going to barge into the bathroom like the police. Samir laughed to himself as he dried off because he knew his friend was probably waiting impatiently outside the door. Leaving the bathroom, Samir walked across the carpeted floor toward the stairs so he could get dressed in his bedroom.

"Man, what the fuck you doin'? I don't know what you on, but the only dick and balls I wanna see is my own! You foul as hell, nigga, and I should beat yo' ass!"

Samir laughed as he accomplished what he set out to do, and that was to make Chade very angry. "Think about this moment when you bring yo' ass to my crib unannounced. I walk around butt ass naked because I live alone, bitch. Oh yeah, thanks for tidying up the place for me," he smirked.

"I got yo' bitch! Kick you square up yo' ass! Selena left yo' ass because she got tired of you smelling like shit. All that hair on yo' ass is not sanitary!" Chade screamed long after Samir was out of sight.

Thirty minutes later, Samir was dressed and ready to go. Standing at six feet, three inches, Samir ran his hand over his goatee then ran a finger over his bushy eyebrows. The black tee and jeans complimented his caramel complexion and hazel eyes. His waves were prominent on top of his head, and Samir loved what he saw reflecting back at him in the mirror. Regardless of his mood, he was going to get up and go to the barbershop. One thing Samir made sure of: never let people have the upper hand to judge his life. So, during his time of sulking, Samir mastered the art of masking how he was really feeling very well.

It had been two months since Selena left and all he'd done in that time frame was worked and brought his ass back home. That day was the first time he would step out of the house in about a week. Samir had taken time off work because his mental mindset was truly fucked up at the moment.

Gathering his keys, phone, and wallet, he left out of the bedroom in search of Chade. Samir looked high and low throughout the house. His friend was nowhere in sight. Something told him to check outside for Chade's vehicle and that was exactly where he found him. Samir locked up the house and walked to the passenger side of the truck and got in.

"Why did you leave the house?" Samir laughed as Chade backed out of the driveway.

"Fuck you, Samir. The shit you pulled coming out of that damn bathroom naked was some homo shit, and I don't appreciate it at all! Save that shit for your wife or your side chick."

Chade knew the moment the words fell from his mouth that he shouldn't have said them. He glanced over at Samir and the humor was no longer on his face. Speaking on his marriage was messed up on Chade's part because he knew how much it pained his friend.

"My bad, man. You gotta make this shit right with Selena before you stress yourself into a stroke. Have you tried to talk to her?"

"There's no talking, bro. The only thing she wants to talk about is Sevyn. I've texted her saying I was willing to go through marriage counseling, and she didn't even respond. Anything I say about our marriage goes on deaf ears. She's gone for good." Samir shook his head and ran his hand down his face in frustration.

"Nah, you're gonna get your family back, fam. Every man has made a mistake by stepping out. Is it right? No, but you can come back from it. All you have to do is show Selena you regret the decision you made and explain what led you to that point. No matter how much you don't want to hurt her feelings, there's nothing you can say that will hurt her more than she's already hurting right now. I believe the reason she's throwing everything y'all worked for to the wolves is because the shit was brought to her attention by someone other than you. I'm going to try my best to help you out. You have to promise you're finished with the other woman though. I mean cut all ties, nigga!"

What Chade said made a lot of sense but it wasn't going to be easy as he was making it out to be. Selena was in her feelings and had every right to feel any way she wanted because Samir had committed the ultimate act of deception. That, for a woman; hell, anyone, was a hard pill to swallow and tarnished a relationship once it was revealed.

"I'm definitely not fuckin' with her anymore. Not saying she doesn't try to interact with me all day at work, but I stop her at every turn. If it's not work-related, I don't address the shit. I've blocked and deleted her from my phone and everything. Lavita is under investigation at work, and I don't want any parts of the crooked shit she was doing. Had I known she was stealing from accounts, I would've never fucked with her on any level. Hopefully, our interactions don't blow up in my face and jeopardize my job."

"Lesson learned. We will figure this thing out later. For now, we're going to enjoy moving furniture with Malik for the remainder of the day," Chade said, keeping his eyes on the road.

"Moving furniture? That's what you got me out the house to do on a Saturday afternoon?" Samir asked irritably.

"It's better than drowning in your sorrows and isolating your-self from the world. Plus, you owe me for cleaning up the pigsty you made of your mancave," Chade shot back. "We're going out for drinks afterwards, so it will be worth it in the end."

Chade had a point, and Samir was glad he had friends that gave a damn about his well-being. Otherwise, he would be ready to end it all, because the thought had crossed his mind a time or two in the past few months. Samir had been sleeping alone, longing for his wife and daughter every second of the day.

Chapter 2

"Selena, when the hell are you going home? I'm tired of you moping around this house like you lost your dog."

Sandra, Selena's mom, was getting on her nerves once again about leaving Samir without trying to work out their marital problems. Her mother loved Samir and, in her eyes, he could do no wrong. Sandra wanted her daughter to go back home and deal with their marriage in private. That was the way things were handled in her mother's house, and she wasn't about to take heed to the bullshit.

"I'm not going home, but if you want me out of your house, I can start looking for a place. As a matter of fact, I'll do just that!"

Selena snatched her phone and started searching for a place for her and Sevyn. She never thought going back home would put more stress on her. Sandra helped with her granddaughter, but every chance she got, she had something to say about the reason Selena was back in her home.

"Now, you know I don't mind you being here. You are my daughter and I will always be here whenever you need me. All I want you to understand is, you are a married woman and your mother's house is not where you should be. For the sake of Sevyn, you and Samir need to talk and reconcile the differences the two of you have with one another."

"Reconcile?" Selena screeched. "Ma, he cheated and stood in my face and lied about it! The evidence was presented, and he still couldn't man up to tell the truth. I'm sorry, I won't allow him to believe cheating is alright. To make matters worse, the bitch playing in my face as if she's gloating about being with my husband. Samir stepped outside of our marriage while I've been nothing but the doting wife to him. My husband chose roadkill out in the street, and he can live with the decision he made. Excuse my language, but fuck Samir!"

Sandra's eyes bucked wide because Selena had never used a curse word in her presence and it took her by surprise. "I understand you are upset and all, but you will not use that type of language around me!" Sandra snapped with her finger pointed in the direction of her daughter. "Yes, Samir cheated. What happened to for better or worse? Selena, that was part of the vows you recited in front of God and all your family and friends."

"You deal with the worse! I'm not putting up with no cheating-ass man! There's no way in hell I'm about to reward him for making me look stupid by going back to him after what the fuck he did to me! No disrespect, but I can't be a younger version of you and my deadbeat-ass father. Breaking the generational curse is a must in my life!"

Sandra flinched as if her daughter slapped her in the face. The truth Selena spoke hurt so much. Sandra couldn't even say she was wrong because then she would be in the wrong for downplaying what was evidently the truth. The shit Sandra had put up with for years and thought her daughter didn't have a clue about was hell. It was painful to see Selena going through her own bout of infidelity in order for her to call her mother out.

"I didn't know you knew about any of the things your father and I endured when you were younger. Why are saying something about it now?"

"How could you assume I didn't know, Ma? There were many nights I would lie awake crying silently along with you as I listened to your sobs. Daddy was nonchalant when you cried about the other women and didn't give a damn about how you felt about it. Then the two of you would make up and wake up the next morning all in love. You never missed a beat catering to that man. Washing his clothes, cooking his meals, and rubbing his damn feet until he decided he wanted to leave for days on end." Selena rolled her eyes as she recalled the events of her parents so called marriage.

"I made a vow to myself that if I ever married, accepting my husband cheating was something I would never do. Being sad all the time, wondering who he was with and when he would return, was never part of my plans as a wife. Long as I am able to get up and go to work every day, I will not sit around acting as if I'm happy when I know for certain that I wasn't. So, again, Samir can kiss my ass. The only thing I want from him is to take care of Sevyn. We don't have to be together in order for him to be a father. There's a thing called co-parenting, and we will both learn how to perfect that shit."

"Selena, I'm going to respect your decision, but I truly believe you are making a huge mistake. Samir is nothing like your father," Sandra said, trying to get Selena to understand.

"But here we are going back and forth about your dear Samir stepping out on our marriage." Selena laughed. "Yeah, they are one and the same. I don't care how you try to dress it up. I'm not turning a blind eye to what happened behind my back. There's no way I'm going to allow my husband to bed hop on my watch," Selena said, heading for the stairs. "Do you mind keeping an eye on Sevyn? I need some air."

"Of course! I got my grandbaby. Go out and have fun. Selena, remember you are still a married woman," Sandra said to her daughter's back as she climbed the stairs.

Selena chuckled. "I'm only married on paper, Mama. In my mind, I'm free to do whatever the hell I choose. My husband did just that without worrying about how it would affect me."

As Selena entered the guest bedroom, she walked over to the closet and snatched a pair of distressed jeans along with a white midriff shirt and threw both items on the bed. The conversation she'd had with her mother replayed in her mind repeatedly, aggravating the hell out of her. Selena knew she owed her mother an apology because the words she spoke had to have pierced her heart profusely in vain.

She shouldn't have thrown her parents' failed marriage in her mother's face the way she had. The truth hurts at all times, but Selena didn't have to use the woman she loved to get her point across. At that moment, she didn't think about how her words would affect her mother. Selena didn't regret speaking her mind though. Maybe that would teach Sandra to let Selena be the grown-ass woman she was.

After showering, Selena walked out of the bathroom and sat on the side of the queen-sized bed. She didn't have a destination in mind when she decided to leave the house. Being inside another minute longer was just not what she wanted to do. Selena still had a couple weeks of maternity days before she went back to work. Her body had snapped back with just a few extra pounds that filled out in the right places; her hips and ass. Admiring her frame in the full-length mirror, Selena smiled because the niggas were about to stop in their tracks, and she didn't plan on telling any of them that she was married.

Her phone rang and Chasity's name appeared on the screen.

"Chasity, what's going on?" Selena asked, placing the phone on speaker to free her hands.

As she moisturized her body, Chasity's voice filled the room. "I haven't heard from you in a minute. Yesterday I called myself surprising you by going to your house, and Samir told me you weren't home. Girl, he looked so sad and disheveled. Is everything alright?"

Selena hated the fact that Chasity went to her house without phoning her beforehand. She hadn't told anyone about what was going on between her and Samir, and she planned to keep it that way. It was no one's business what was happening in her home.

"Everything is just fine." Selena left her response short and sweet. The line was quiet for a few seconds before Chasity snickered. "What's funny?" Selena asked as her hand paused on her thigh.

"Why are you trying to keep shit secret? Samir already told me you left him. Tell me what happened."

Samir didn't tell her messy ass shit. He couldn't stand to hear the mention of her name, let alone telling her about what was going on between the two of them. Chasity was trying to see if Selena would let her in on what was going on in her life.

Since things went left with her and Ahmad, Chasity didn't want to see anyone happy if she wasn't. She tried for weeks to win Ahmad over to give her another chance, but he wasn't trying to hear anything Chasity had to say. One thing the experience didn't do was shut down her respiratory system. She was too strong for that shit. Chasity went right back to social media and filled her bag back up. She had a few potentials in her sights, so it was business as usual.

A gold-digger stopped at nothing to get the funds needed to maintain the lifestyle they were accustomed to.

"I don't owe you an explanation about why I wasn't home when you went there unannounced. Samir didn't tell you shit because there's nothing to tell, with your nosy ass. Did you call to get into the happenings of my life? If so, you're worried about the wrong shit, because everything is good over here."

"Your defensiveness already let me know there's trouble in paradise, sweetie. The shit was bound to happen. Hell, he's Ahmad's friend. None of them niggas are worth a damn," Chasity laughed.

"Chasity, you're still salty about Ahmad seeing you for the grimy bitch you are. I would never be sad and lonely like your ass because I still have a husband. Believe me, Selena and Samir are good over here."

"Girl, bye! I bet that nigga cheated and now you know your pussy couldn't keep his ass at home. Your daughter ain't even a year old," Chasity laughed again. "I told you he would leave soon as you had that baby."

Selena hung up before she got too mad and disclosed to Chasity that there was in fact, trouble in paradise. Her words were venomous and cut deep. Selena blocked Chasity's number, but really wanted to find her and whoop her ass. Instead, Selena decided to hit a bar and have a couple drinks; alone.

After getting dressed, Selena pulled her long hair into a ponytail and applied a light coat of gloss on her lips. She looked in the mirror as she slipped her feet into a pair of classic white Chucks. Selena was satisfied with her appearance and ready to hit the California streets. Saying goodbye to her mother, she kissed Sevyn and made her way out of the house to her car that was parked in the driveway.

Driving aimlessly, around trying to figure out where she was going, Selena thought about all she'd been through. Tears filled her eyes as an image of her husband sexing a woman that wasn't her flashed in her mind. The muscles in his back constricted with every stroke of his hips. Selena shook her head and focused back on the road just in time to slam on the brakes. The screeching of the tires scared the shit out of her as the car slowed, but didn't stop in time to avoid hitting the back of a Porsche 718 Boxster.

"Fuck!" Selena screamed as she threw the car in park and got out. She examined the damage and wondered how the hell she hit the back of a parked car. The expensive car had a small dent in the bumper and there was paint and a dent on Selena's front end. "This is bullshit! How did I hit this damn car?" she cried as she walked to the driver's side of the Porsche. No one was inside.

Bad as Selena wanted to get back in her car and drive off, her conscience wouldn't allow her to do so. Instead, she went to her purse and grabbed an envelope to write a note for the owner. Selena thought about the cost of damage to the luxury vehicle and cringed.

Good evening, my name is Selena Jamison. I accidentally hit your vehicle. My phone number is (424) 555-0319, feel free to give me a call so we can exchange insurance information to handle the damage. I'm so sorry for any trouble I have caused.

Selena sighed deeply as she walked slowly to put the note under the windshield wiper. Once she was back at her vehicle, she glanced at the damage once more before getting into the driver's seat and drove off. A couple blocks down the street she noticed a sports bar and decided to go in for a much-needed drink.

"Good evening, ma'am. Would you like a table, booth, or a seat at the bar?" the hostess asked.

"I'll take a booth, please."

Following the hostess to the middle of the establishment, Selena was still thinking about ruining the beautiful vehicle. For some, the damage was minor, but she knew how outrageous the prices were for cars of that caliber. It was nothing to get the dent and paint off of her Nissan Maxima, but she couldn't say the same for the owner of the Porsche. As she sat inside the booth, Selena automatically picked up the menu to order an appetizer to go with her drink.

A waitress walked over right away with a pad in hand along with a bright smile. "Can I start you out with a drink?" she asked cheerfully.

"Yes, I will take a Long Island, very little ice, with an order of spinach dip and chips, please."

"I'll be right back with your drink. It will be a few minutes for the dip and chips."

"That's fine. Thank you," Selena replied.

As soon as Selena was alone, the tears flowed down her face. She put her head down on her arms and sobbed silently. The vibration of her phone forced her to compose herself. There was a text message from Samir and Selena really didn't trust herself to open it. After a few minutes, she pushed the selfishness aside and read the message.

Hubby: Babe, it's been months and I miss you and Sevyn. Please, allow me to right my wrong. I'm so sorry for stepping out on our marriage and hurting you. I love you, Selena. Living without you have been hell. Our house is just not a home without my family.

Selena wanted to forgive Samir with everything in her, but everything her mother accepted from her father didn't stop him from stepping out on her. To her, it gave him the greenlight to continue doing the shit because she didn't put a stop to his bullshit. If Selena's father hadn't left for another woman, Sandra would've still been going through hell. Samir was never going to get a second chance to shit on her in public.

Hearing her mother cry when she was younger after being put to bed still pained Selena, even before Samir's infidelity. The difference between then and now was that Sevyn was too young to understand her mother's pain. Anger replaced the hurt and Selena allowed the hurt to respond to her husband's message.

Wifey: Believe it or not, I miss you too, Samir. I'll be damned if I let that deter me into believing you're sorry for fucking another bitch! You jeopardized your marriage to wet the next hoe's ass then come home to me! Fuck you, Samir! I won't put on blinders and pretend what happened didn't occur! I've been nothing but good to you and instead of talking about whatever drove you to another woman's arms, you decided to go out and live life as if you were single, leaving me home to struggle through my pain alone. I'm done! I want a divorce and that's all there is to it.

Samir responded back immediately, but before Selena could read whatever he had to say, her phone rang with a number she didn't recognize. Selena contemplated not answering, then remembered she'd wrecked someone's car. Wiping the tears from her eyes, she answered the call.

"Hello?"

"Yeah, may I speak with Selena Jamison?"

The deep baritone that flowed through the airways caused Selena to lose her train of thought. Her tongue was stuck to the roof of her mouth, preventing her speaking once she snapped out of the trance she was in temporarily.

"Are you still there?" he snapped.

"Yes. Yes, I'm still here. This is Selena. How may I help you?"

"This is Hayden Vick. You left a message on my car today."

Nervousness took over Selena's body because Mr. Vick sounded upset once she identified herself. He had every right to be, since Selena did, in fact, damage his vehicle. Taking a deep breath, she swallowed a couple times to moisten her dry mouth. There wasn't anything she could do other than apologize to the man for the troubles she may have caused.

"I'm sorry for not paying attention to where I was going. No one showed up as I waited for someone to claim the car. I wasn't running away from what I had done."

"Where are you now? We need to exchange information so I can get my shit fixed."

The tone of Hayden's voice shook Selena to the core. She was kind of afraid to tell him where she actually was at the moment. Selena looked around the bar and it was pretty full, so that alone made her feel a sense of security. There was no way he would be stupid enough to get violent with so many witnesses. She understood why he was upset because had someone hit her car, anger would be the exact emotion she would've held as well.

"I'm at Macio's Sports Bar. It's on—"

"I know exactly where it is. I'll see you in five," he said, ending the call.

At that precise moment, the waitress brought her drink and spinach dip and placed them in front of Selena. She muttered a thank you and was left alone to enjoy her appetizer and drink. Selena took

22

a long gulp of the Long Island and clutched her throat. The liquid was stronger than she thought it would be. Setting the glass on the right of her, Selena took a couple bites of the spinach dip and chips before opening the message from Samir.

Hubby: See, you're talking crazy right now. We need to sit down and talk this shit out, Selena. I know what I did was wrong, but divorce is not the answer. Our daughter needs both of her parents in the same household. Please don't do this, baby. I'll do whatever it takes to show you how much I love you.

Hayden walked into the bar and looked around, trying to figure out which woman was Selena Jamison. When he couldn't figure it out, he took his phone out and called her while still browsing. Hayden zoomed in on a woman sitting by herself in a booth. She was looking around nervously before glancing down at her phone. Making his way across the establishment, he ended the call before it connected. As he got closer, it seemed as if she let out a huge sigh of relief.

"Selena?" he asked, sitting across from her without waiting for confirmation. "I'm Hayden."

Selena placed her purse on the table and started rambling through the contents of the bag. Never lifting her head, she slid the insurance card towards him along with her license. "You can take a picture with your phone and take care of your business."

A lone tear escaped her eye. She tried to swipe it away before Hayden could catch the gesture. It didn't work because all the anger dissipated from his face once he saw how beautiful she was. Selena had high cheekbones that chiseled her face perfectly and a set of round lips that looked soft and plump. You know, the kind that a man would love to kiss nonstop for the rest of his life. She had a set of China-like eyes, but the rims were red from crying.

"Selena, look at me," Hayden said softly. Selena shook her head, continuing to look inside her purse. "I'm sorry if I came off harshly over the phone. It seems like you hitting my ride should've been the least of your worries. There's something much heavier on your mind. You want to talk about it? I have time."

Hayden stared as Selena continued to dig around inside her purse. She never pulled anything out and he figured she was avoiding looking at him. Taking in her demeanor was like Hayden watching his mother cry over his father walking out on her years prior. As she set her bag on the side of her, the ring on her left ring finger sparkled under the light. That made Hayden sigh lowly because it never crossed his mind that Selena was a taken woman. All he saw was her beauty hidden behind the pain she was carrying within her.

"Look, don't worry about the damage costs. Your honesty holds enough weight for me to forgive you for what happened today. My main concern right now is to make sure you're going to be okay."

"I'm fine. Thanks for the offer, but I'm all for paying my debt. I can't allow you to pay for something I did because I was deep in my thoughts and not paying attention to where I was going."

"Come on now, you don't have to bear this burden alone. Think of me as a friend that's willing to hear you out. Let it out, ma. Holding shit in will have you stroking out."

Selena sat quietly with her chin tucked into her chest. When she lifted her head, her eyes were filled to the brim and the tears flowed effortlessly down her face. Hayden pushed her documents across the table toward her and waited for her to speak. Instead, she grabbed her glass and took a hefty drink from the straw. Wiping her eyes, Selena folded her hands in front of her dip then pushed it away.

"There's nothing to really talk about. As you may have noticed, I'm a married woman and there's trouble in paradise. This too shall pass," she said, taking another sip of her drink.

"Every marriage has its ups and down. You must have faith and it will get better. Trust me, I've been there."

Selena chuckled and shook her head no. "Nah, he can do better without me because I'm done. It only takes one time to cheat on me. I won't be the woman that sits back and lets the shit happen a second and third time. Obviously, I wasn't enough for him to tell the bitch to kick rocks. He made his bed, now he must lie in it."

24

"I understand where you're coming from. If there are children involved, you have to take them into consideration. Kids nowadays need their fathers, especially boys."

"To be frank with you, Hayden, my daughter is the reason I made the decision to leave. She is seven months, and her father will still be part of her life. Just not with me. We will have to get that co-parent thing down pat because I'm riding solo. First thing Monday morning, I'll be filing for divorce."

"Now, do you really want to do that without trying to work things out first? I mean, that's what counseling is for, Selena. What happened to for better or worse?" Selena's eyes turned to slits as she glared at Hayden. "Whoa, I'm just saying," he said, throwing his hands up in surrender.

"You sound like my mother, and I'm not going for any of that. Did he think about counseling when he was fucking the next bitch?" Selena asked with her head tilted to the side. "Didn't think so. Like I said, I'm done."

She drank the rest of her Long Island before grabbing her purse and scooting out of the booth. She stood beside the table with her hand held out to shake Hayden's. He placed his hand into her outstretched one and stood as well.

"I will be giving you a call sometime Monday after I take care of my business so we can get the damage of your car squared away."

"I told you that won't be necessary, Selena." The look in her eyes made Hayden retract his statement and agree with her. Nodding his head with a smile, he replied, "I'll be waiting on your call."

"Waiting on her call for what?" Samir's voice boomed through the establishment.

Hayden stepped back because he knew shit was about to hit the fan.

Meesha

Chapter 3

Samir and the gang finally finished arranging the furniture and desks in Toni's paralegal firm. The job was rough, but they got it done. Now everyone was hungry and just wanted to relax with a few drinks. The group of friends walked into Macio's and waited to be seated. Samir looked around to see how crowded it was so they'd have a general idea how long the wait would be. The bar wasn't too busy and at that moment, the hostess walked over to them.

"How many is in your party?"

"Six," Ahmad replied, sizing the woman up from head to toe. She blushed as she turned to take them to a table large enough for all of them.

Samir stopped in his tracks, causing Malik to bump into his back. He was ready to curse his boy out, but when he noticed the tight clutch of his hands, he knew they were about to move some more furniture, but they might end up in jail for fucking up the establishment. Samir took long strides toward the middle of the bar and all eyes were on him. Malik and Sanji noticed what was about to go down and they damn near ran behind their friend before he killed Selena's ass.

"Wait on her call for what?"

Samir never took his eye off the nigga standing with his wife's hand in his. Hayden backed up and Selena didn't even attempt to turn around. She rolled her eyes as she tried her best to calm herself because anger had started to raise her body temperature. The last thing Selena wanted was to cause a bigger scene than the one her husband had already started. Even though the meeting with Hayden was innocent, Samir didn't have a right to ride down on her in the manner he'd done. He was the one that cheated, and he had the nerve to be jealous because he saw another man in her presence. Bad as she wanted to laugh in his face, she didn't.

"Can't nobody talk now, huh? It seemed like there was a lot being said while I was walking up. Somebody better say something before I beat this muthafucka's ass in this bitch!" Samir sneered.

"Man, this ain't what you think," Hayden finally said.

"Don't explain shit to him! I'm his wife, and he should direct his bullshit at me, not you," Selena said, turning to face Samir. "I advise you to go enjoy the rest of your day with the homies, because you don't have a leg to stand on to question me about anything," Selena hissed.

"You crazy as hell if you think that shit! You're my wife, or have you forgotten that tad bit of information?" Samir asked with a raised eyebrow.

"I'm only your wife for the moment, Samir. You ended the marriage when you broke the vows we made to one another. Do you hear me ranting and raving about that every second of the day? No, because I packed my things and eliminated myself from the equation. It's beneath me now. Trust, if I was seeing this man right here, you would know about it. Stay in your fuckin' lane before I embarrass your ass in here."

Selena sidestepped her husband and walked toward the exit. She had nothing else to say to Samir about the matter. Little did she know, Samir was hot on her heels, because he wasn't finished talking to her. When she reached for the handle of her car door, she opened it and it was slammed back forcibly.

"What the fuck are you doing, Selena, and where is my daughter?"

Selena looked around before responding to his hostile attitude. "She's with my mother. You are free to go pick her up for the rest of the weekend. What I have going on is none of your business," Selena snapped back. "She should be your only concern at this point. You're worried about the wrong shit right now."

"Regardless of what you may think, I'm still your husband. Don't get that nigga beat the fuck up, Selena."

Samir was breathing like a dragon, but his actions didn't move his wife one bit. The door to the bar opened and Hayden stepped out at the wrong time. Samir's head turned and the fire in his eyes turned into infrared beams.

"Aye, homie, what's your dealings with my wife?" Samir asked, folding his arms over his chest. The door opened again and all of his friends stepped out to make sure he was good. "You were aware that she is a married woman, right?"

"Like I was trying to tell yo' hot-tempered ass inside, it's not what you think. Mrs. Jamison and I are not involved in any way. She shot me her location after leaving a note on my car because she ran into the back of my shit. Now, since you want to puff out your chest over nothing, get ready to pay for the damages, *Husband.* I'll be waiting on your call, Mrs. Jamison," Hayden said, walking to his car and peeling out of the parking lot.

Samir stared at Selena, but she just shook her head and opened the door of her car for the second time. Selena paused then turned to Samir. She looked him in the eyes with pure hate. "I'll have Sevyn ready when you're ready for her. Call before you come. Don't pop up at my mama's house." With that, Selena got in her vehicle and drove off without another word.

Everybody made their way back into the building and Samir wanted to ask them for a raincheck, but with the way Chade found him, there was no way they would allow him to leave. Seeing Selena with another man did something to Samir's mental. The last message she sent played in his mind and he couldn't believe she threw the word divorce at him. There was no way Selena was willing to end their union over one damn mistake.

After sitting at the table, Samir ordered two double shots of Remy and a Corona. The guys gave their drink orders, then Sanji cleared his throat, bringing all the attention his way.

"Samir, I know how you're feeling, fam. Selena is hurt right now, and you have to give her space to think everything out. If you keep coming at her like you are, she's going to bounce on your ass for sure. You have to think about what put y'all in this predicament, man."

Samir's eyebrows furrowed as he glared at his friend. What Sanji said was true, but he didn't do all this shit on his own. Yeah, he stepped out on his marriage, but the consequences behind it were partially Selena's fault. Did it justify his actions? No. At the same time, he was still a man and had needs that his wife wasn't willing to handle.

"What about the shit she put me through during her pregnancy? The last couple of months were the hardest. I did every fuckin' thing I could to be by her side, and she pushed me away. I'm not blaming Selena for my infidelities, but she played a part in the shit. What man do you know that's getting turned down by his own wife gon' walk around the house with blue balls?"

"You were supposed to go in the bathroom and choke that muthafucka 'til he spit in yo' hand! The fuck you thought, nigga?" Malik angrily responded. "Selena ain't yo' girlfriend. She's your wife. The rules changed when you put a ring on her finger and committed to her. No other woman should've had your attention, sexually or otherwise. We're not in college no more, man. If you were that unhappy, you should've talked to her about the shit y'all was going through. Prenatal depression is real. Many women experience depression during their pregnancies. The changes of their bodies, mood swings, and all is capable of bringing on depression. Take it from me being a doctor. I know firsthand. I see it every day."

His boys weren't playing the "we're on your side" shit with Samir. They were giving it to him raw and uncut. He couldn't do anything other than listen to them and plead his case when he felt the need to do so. They were all pissed in some shape, form, or fashion about what Samir had done, but there was no way he could make the shit disappear. Samir threw the shot back and chased it with his beer and just tapped his fingers on the table.

"We coming down on you hard because you are the only one out of the bunch that's married. Yes, Malik and I are engaged, but all that hopping from woman-to-woman shit is dead. Once you get in the mindset of going in another direction other than the one with your wife, there's a simple solution to that. Leave her the fuck alone! I hear what you're saying about her not wanting to be bothered while she was pregnant. I get it. That shit with ole girl shouldn't have made it back to your home front."

"Chade, I know Baylei changed you for the better and I appreciate y'all speaking up, but this is my marriage and it's hurting me and Selena at the moment. Y'all are just on the outside looking in.

Nobody knows exactly how I feel not having my family under the same roof with me, man. I fucked up."

"Like Sanji said, bro, you have to give her time. Selena said she wanted a divorce and she probably do. You have to be strong for Sevyn and get yourself ready for whatever she throws at you. Trying to strong arm her into being with you will only cause her to become bitter. You definitely don't want that," Vincent said, patting Samir on the back.

They sat back shooting the shit as they drank a couple more rounds before Samir got up so he could go pick up his baby girl. His heart was hollow as he thought about how things would play out with Selena. They had been together six years, married three, and he was on the trail back to being a single man. That shit didn't sit well with him. Saying a silent praying to the man upstairs to save his marriage, Samir drove in silence to face his wife.

***

The time Samir got to spend with his daughter was bittersweet. Hearing her coo, cry, and fuss brought joy back into his life. For the most part, he loved on her while she was awake and cried as he watched her sleep. Knowing he would be taking her back to Selena hurt him in more ways than one. Samir didn't know how he would function in the home alone after Sevyn left. The baby sounds and smells would go away in a matter of days and he didn't want that. In the back of his mind, he wanted to tell Selena to kiss his ass because he needed his baby. The words his friends spoke resonated in his mind and he got up to do the right thing.

After taking a shower, he walked into the nursery to check on Sevyn and she was still sleeping soundly. Samir took the opportunity to get dressed for work so he could get the baby ready to head out. He had to drop Sevyn off and go to work from there. Samir was out of the house about forty-five minutes later with plenty of time to stop and grab something to eat.

He called Selena to let her know he was down the street. She was standing on the porch when he pulled up. Samir watched as she descended the steps and jumped out to help with the baby. She was too fast because she had the bag over her shoulder and the car seat out by the time he could make a move to assist. Muttering a good morning, Selena was heading back to the house.

"You can't wait a minute to talk?" Samir asked, leaning against the side of his car.

"There's nothing to talk about, Samir. You had the chance to speak your truth, and you lied. It doesn't matter now."

"Were you serious about the divorce?" Samir walked behind his wife and her shoulders became stiff as a board.

"Serious as a heart attack. You hurt me and it's inexcusable, Samir. There's no coming back from that type of deception." Selena turned to face him with tears in her eyes. "Why wasn't I enough, Samir? You know what? Don't even answer that. I'll be going to the courthouse soon as I contact Mr. Vick about the damage to his vehicle."

"Selena, our daughter needs both of us in her life right now. You know how it feels to live without your father. Why would you want our daughter to grow up that way?"

Anger replaced the pain in her eyes as she sat the car seat on the top step along with the bag. "That exactly why I'm going through with my decision. My daddy did my mama dirty as hell and thought because she didn't leave, it gave him the green light to keep fucking over her. I'm not going through that mess, Samir. You got your one strike. There won't be a second or a third. Sevyn is going to be fine. One thing I can say, you are a great father to our daughter, and I doubt if you will turn your back on her like my daddy did me. You're not built like that."

The tears ran down her face like a waterfall and it tugged at Samir's heartstrings. Reaching out to wipe them away, Selena jerked her head back and swiped them away quickly. *Damn, she doesn't even want me to touch her*, Samir said to himself. Shaking his head, he removed his wallet from his pocket and handed her several bills so she could pay the nigga for his car.

"This should be enough to give dude for his car. I have to get to work. Would it be okay if I come see Sevyn when I get off?"

"Samir, you can come see or get her whenever you want. One thing I won't do is keep you away from our daughter. When I find a place, I will be sure to let you know. Until then, we will be right here. All I ask is that you call before you show up."

"Find a place?" Samir asked with an attitude. You have a whole fuckin' house that I bought for your ass!" *Give her time, fam. That's all you can do.* Pinching the bridge of his nose with his eyes closed, Samir opened his eyes and stared at his wife. "I'm sorry, Selena. Whatever you feel you gotta do, make it happen. I love you."

Without uttering a word, Selena gathered the baby and her diaper bag, leaving Samir standing at the bottom of the stairs as she entered the house, slamming the door behind her. Samir stood staring at the closed door long after his wife disappeared. It took everything in him not to go after her. Letting her have the time she needed wasn't going to be as easy for him as it was for her.

Twenty minutes later, Samir was walking into his place of employment, and the tension was thick. Tellers were eyeing him as he passed by and the normal good mornings were mere mumbles. Something was going on, and he had no clue what he was walking into. The not knowing was killing Samir, but he was going to find out what was going on soon enough.

Walking into his office, Samir placed his briefcase on the desk and proceeded to take his suit jacket off before turning on his computer. There was a light knock on the door and he froze in place. The door opened before he could invite whomever was on the other side to enter. His boss, Mr. Whittaker peeked around the door with a grim expression on his face.

"Mr. Jamison, good morning. I need you to meet me in the conference room in the next ten minutes. Don't ask any questions. Just show up on time."

With that, he left the same way he entered. Samir grabbed his jacket and made his way to the conference room to get whatever Mr. Whittaker had planned out of the way. Entering the conference room, sweat started forming under his armpits the moment he laid eyes on Lavita sitting on the far end of the table. There was a television set up at the head of the table with a folder sitting on top of it. Samir kind of had an idea what was going on at that point and figured he was summoned to be a witness. Lavita cut her eyes at him and pursed her lips before turning her head. She was breathing heavily with her arms folded over her chest.

"Good morning, Miss Levitt."

"Fuck you, Samir," she gritted. "I have never been *Miss Levitt* to you. Stop fronting and call me Vita like you did when your hands were massaging my ass while I rode that big dick. Don't play with me, nigga! What the fuck are we here for?"

"I don't know why we are here. Lavita, what we have done outside of this building needs to stay that way. Are we understood?"

"Fuck that. If this is about what I think it's about, I won't be the only one being escorted out of this muthafucka. Believe that shit," she smirked.

Her face became stoic when Mr. Whittaker entered the room with another man and a woman. Samir took a seat away from Lavita and waited patiently for the meeting to begin. The woman wore a name tag that read M. Tucker and the guy's read S. Pulaski. Who they were was a mystery, because Samir had never seen them before. Lavita was shifting in her seat and beads of sweat were forming on her forehead. Mr. Whittaker cleared his throat as he unbuttoned his suit jacket and snatched the folder from its position.

"Good morning, Miss Levitt. I'm Mr. Whittaker, the Managing Director here at Wells Fargo. How long have you been an employee with us?" he asked with his hands steepled firmly together.

"Um, I started working for the company five years ago, but have been at this location for two." Lavita was short and straight to the point with her response.

"From what we've gathered, you have done an excellent job in the timeframe that you've been with us. A raise would surely be in your future when the time comes." Mr. Whittaker smiled. Lavita squared her shoulders and sat up straight giving a slight head nod.

"Thank you so much. I really appreciate you taking notice of how seriously I pride myself in doing a great job."

The smile fell from Mr. Whittaker's face. Agent Tucker's head snapped in Lavita's direction quickly and Samir adjusted the collar of his shirt because shit was starting to get hot. Lavita shifted nervously in her seat as all eyes were on her, including Samir's. The rustling of papers was the only sound in the room.

"Miss Levitt," Miss Tucker paused as she scanned a document in front of her. "Is your ID number LL0908000?"

"You know that's my ID number. Get on with the reason I'm being interrogated like a criminal," Lavita snapped.

"Okay, I'm going to cut to the chase. There's no need for any attitude. Agent Pulaski and I are here from the FBI to investigate a series of complaints that have come across the desk of Mr. Whittaker."

Lavita's eyes bulged out of the sockets as she listened to the words spoken. Samir turned slightly in his seat to get a good look at her reaction. Even though he knew Lavita was under investigation, Samir didn't know it was at the extent of the FBI being involved. Losing her job was one thing, but things might be heading toward jail time.

"Dating back two years, there were small withdrawals that weren't detected at the time, but after further investigation, it was found that all of the transactions were completed by *you*, Miss Levitt," Agent Tucker revealed.

"I—I—don't—" Lavita stuttered before she was ordered to remain silent until directed to speak.

"In the span of two months, there was approximately $350,000 illegally withdrawn from three prominent accounts. The problem lies with you, Miss Levitt, because all of them were transferred or distributed by you. Would you care to explain who gave the authorization for these transactions?"

Hearing Agent Tucker run down the information they had on Lavita stunned Samir. Lavita didn't live the life of someone who would have the quarter million dollars said to be stolen. She lived in the hood of L.A. and drove a car that wasn't considered luxurious. She was definitely facing jail time based off the line of questioning being thrown at her. The agents had all the proof they needed to put Lavita behind bars. Her best bet was to tell the truth and leave nothing out. Samir looked on tight-lipped, waiting for

Lavita's explanation about the accusations against her. She sat biting her bottom lip without attempting to speak.

"We're waiting, Miss Levitt," Mr. Whittaker snarled.

Lavita's facial expression went from scared to menacing, like the damn Chucky doll in the movie *Child's Play*. It was as if the devil came from hell to tear shit up on earth. She leaned forward on the table and folded her hands in front of her looking Agent Tucker directly in her eyes.

"So, let me get this straight," Lavita said, clearing her throat. "All the documentation you have in the folder before you has my ID number on every single one of them, correct?" Both agents nodded their heads in agreement. "See, that's not possible because when we are busy, there are times when other tellers jump in and take over if a teller is trying to complete another task, such as, taking money to the vault or getting change for someone."

All eyes went to Samir for confirmation. He didn't notice because his focus was on Lavita and the lie she had told. There was no way Lavita was about to jeopardize his job in the manner she was trying to do at that moment. Even though he wasn't the only manager working at the bank, he was the only one included in the meeting that day, and he had to set the record straight on her allegation.

"That's not true at all. Under no circumstances is any teller allowed to work on another's till. Everyone is responsible for their own bank and must sign in with their log-in and log out whenever they leave the station. If it has ever happened, I was never aware of it."

Lavita didn't appreciate Samir going against her and siding with the very people who were trying to sabotage her career. She sat back in her chair, biting her tongue before she said something that would further incriminate herself.

Mr. Whittaker stood from his seat and pressed the button to turn on the television. On the screen was a still image of Lavita greeting a customer with a smile. The play button was activated and the video started playing.

In the video, Lavita was seen interacting with a male customer that was withdrawing money. The time and date were stamped in the lower right corner of the screen. It took about five minutes for Lavita to complete the transaction. The customer left with what appeared to be a check or a money order, and Lavita watched him until he was safely out of the bank. The video played, showing her wiping the top of her lip and looking around suspiciously before calling over the next customer. Mr. Whittaker paused the video, allowing Agent Pulaski to address Lavita.

"Miss Levitt, do you personally know that guy in the video?" He asked rewinding the footage,

"No. I don't think he's a regular because I can't recall his name."

Agent Pulaski stared at the footage then down at the paper in front of him. "His name is Steven Wyatt, correct?"

The room became extremely hot as Lavita fought to find the correct words to the agent's question. Steven Wyatt was a wealthy businessman that frequented the bank. Everyone knew who he was because he made it his business to get to know all the employees because he showed his appreciation for their work every Christmas. She was beating her own ass for not going with her first mind and leaving the man's money alone. She didn't think Mr. Wyatt would even notice the fifty thousand she'd stolen from him was missing. The man had millions in his savings and ten times more in his checking.

"No, that's not Mr. Wyatt. Everyone knows who he is," Lavita responded truthfully.

"The cashier's check you presented to Mr. Walker, the man in the video, had Mr. Wyatt's name on it. He came back a week later and cashed that very check and *you*, Miss Levitt were the teller that gave him fifty thousand dollars of Mr. Wyatt's money; in cash. Do you remember that day?"

Lavita had nothing to say about the matter because she was caught red-handed and opted to keep her mouth closed. Evan had held on to the money until she got off work, and she hit him with ten grand for doing the job with her. If the FBI knew of his involvement, that only meant he was already in custody and she was next.

"I think it would be best if I didn't say anything else. I would like to speak with a lawyer before I go any further with this," Lavita said in a shaky voice.

"Very well, Miss Levitt. You have a right to remain silent…"

Agent Tucker read Lavita her Miranda rights as she walked around the table while removing handcuffs from her waist. Reality kicked in for Lavita and the waterworks started the minute she was asked to stand. As the cold steel clasped around her wrist, thoughts of Samir blocking her calls, not having sex with her anymore, and choosing his wife over her flooded her mind. If she was going down, Lavita was taking his ass right along with her.

"Wait, I have a confession to make," Lavita blurted out when her arm was snatched behind her back. "Mr. Jamison instructed me on how to get the money without being detected! He was the mastermind behind all of this! You have to believe me!"

Samir looked at Lavita like the crazy bitch she was and wanted to slap the fuck out of her, but going to jail was something he wasn't trying to do. He shook his head no in Mr. Whittaker's direction, and his boss held his hand up to stop Samir from speaking on the matter. When Lavita realized her outburst went on death ears, she became furious."

"Tell them how you fucked me in every hole God blessed me with, motherfucker! Tell them how we would leave this building and go up the street on our lunch break to have wild, steamy sex before coming back until we clocked out at six! Be a man and let them know you are not the respectable man they think you are, Samir! You are the husband that has a wife at night and on the weekends, with a whole side bitch during the work day! Tell them!"

Samir shook his head because the shit Lavita revealed had nothing to do with the fact that she stole money and got caught. He knew there was nothing to implicate him in her money-laundering scheme and she lowkey knew it as well. That was the reason she was trying to tell the world he was breaking her back and cut her off. Now she was bitter about it. Mr. Whittaker was shooting daggers at Samir, but he had to keep a straight face and continue to be silent. Lavita was escorted from the premises in handcuffs and she was still screaming Samir's name the entire time.

Mr. Whittaker had a look of disappointment on his face and instructed Samir to sit so they could talk. *If I lose my job behind that bitch, I'm beating her ass soon as I catch up with her,* Samir said to himself as he did what he was told.

Meesha

Chapter 4

Selena left the house a few hours after Samir and headed to the address of the mechanic shop where Hayden's car was being serviced. He sent the address when she texted him earlier that morning. Hayden told Selena he would contact her when the car was ready and she didn't have to go in to pay just yet. Selena wasn't trying to hear what he said because she wanted to get the payment out of the way as soon as possible.

As she followed the directions of the GPS, thoughts of her marriage swarmed her mind. Hearing Samir profess his love for her almost broke her down and opened the door to forgive him, but the image of him sexing someone else pushed the thought right back out.

When she pulled into the parking lot, there were quite a few cars lined up along the service area. All Selena wanted to do was go inside and pay for the damages she'd caused.

Selena sat in her car for a minute before cutting the ignition. She got out of her vehicle and walked slowly to the entrance of the shop. Every eye was on her as she waltzed inside, patiently waiting in line. The woman behind the counter was doing a great job getting every customer situated in a timely manner. When Selena finally made it to the counter, she was greeted with much professionalism.

"Welcome to Nitty's Auto Repair. How may I help you?"

"Yes, I'm here to see Frank. Is he available?" Selena asked.

"He's on an important call at the moment. Maybe I can be of assistance?"

"No. I'll wait until he's available. Would you please inform him that Selena Jamison is here to see him, please?"

The expression on the woman's face displayed displeasure as she slowly lifted the receiver from the base. Selena stepped back to allow the next person in line to approach the counter. Feeling eyes on her, Selena turned in the direction of the woman and noticed the prominent scowl she wore. Her entire approach towards the man in front of her was different than the last two customers. The

41

pleasantries were gone, and Selena didn't know where the distain from the woman came from or why.

A few moments later a tall, dark-skinned, handsome guy with a low-cut fade walked into the room from the back. His arura screamed Boss without him uttering a word. As he passed some of the patrons, they greeted him with utmost respect and in return, he shook hands while throwing head nods at others. Selena found herself enthralled in his handsomeness, causing her to get lost in a world of her own.

"Andrea, who is the person here to see me?" the man Selena had sexed with her eyes asked.

"That one over there," she said, throwing her thumb in Selena's direction before she went back to assisting the man before her.

Selena blinked a couple times to regain focus. Frank licked his lips while running his hand down the front of his St. Laurent T-shirt. The muscles in his chest hugged the hell out of the material. His arms were covered in tattoos. The artwork on display told a story only Frank could tell. Clearing his throat, Frank rubbed his hands together looking down on Selena. His six-foot frame towered over her short one and he liked what he saw in the woman standing await.

"Hello, I'm Frank. What can I do for you, Beautiful?"

"Um." Selena cleared her throat as she tried to remember why she came into Nitty's Auto Repair. She shifted from one foot to the other before gathering her thoughts. "I'm sorry. My name is Selena and I've come to pay the bill on behalf of Hayden Vick."

Frank had a look of confusion on his face for a moment, but he snapped into business mode fairly quickly. Excusing himself, he walked behind the counter and spoke lowly to the woman who had given Selena attitude. Typing away on the keyboard the woman handed Frank a single sheet of paper from the printer. As he made moved to walk back in Selena's direction, the woman's words stopped him in his tracks.

"Make sure you keep that shit all about business, Nitty," she snapped.

"Mind the business I pay you, Tasha, and stay out of mine," he retorted, walking away from her.

Selena stood waiting for Frank to make his way back to her. She was ready to pay and be on her way because she was hungry. Her stomach felt as if it was touching her back. She stayed up all night looking over some of the photos her assistant had done while she'd been away. After seeing the images, Selena decided it was time for her to get back into the workforce to keep her mind off what she was going through with Samir. Photography had always been her passion and she had made a career of it and opened her own studio before she walked down the aisle to be married.

"I'm sorry about that. It looks as if Mr. Vick paid his balance in full. There must've been some type of misunderstanding."

Selena frowned because Hayden told Samir to pay up and he did just that. She wasn't going to worry about it because the money would be used for Sevyn. Selena appreciated Samir for even stepping up to settle her debt after she walked away from their marriage.

"You did a number on his whip." Frank laughed, showing his perfect white teeth. "I can see why he wrote the damages off as a loss though. You're beautiful. How can I get to know you better, Selena?"

"Thank you," she blushed, lifting her left hand to show the princess cut diamond ring resting on her finger. "Unfortunately, I'm a married woman, Frank." At that precise moment, Selena's stomach growled loudly and embarrassed the hell out of her.

"Was that your stomach?" he asked, wide-eyed.

Selena's face turned beet red as she nodded her head, laughing nervously. "I didn't eat breakfast this morning. I'm going to head out. Thank you so much for helping me out today."

"Let me take you out to eat. I would hate for you to get light-headed and crash out there on the road." Selena shook her head no as she took a step to leave his establishment. "It would be just lunch. I promise. Just two adults going out to eat. Straight platonic shit." Frank smiled.

Selena's stomach growled again and Frank sprang into action. "Tasha, I'll be back. I'm going to lunch."

The woman threw her hand at Frank and kept assisting the customer standing before her. Frank gently grabbed her arm and led

Selena toward the door. He wasn't taking no for an answer. Selena headed to her car and hit the locks on the key fob. Frank halted her steps as she neared her vehicle.

"You can leave your car here and ride with me."

"Nah, that's okay. I'll follow behind so I won't have to double back to get home."

Frank nodded his head as he glanced at the front of her car. Seeing the minor damage, he took note and estimated the cost in his head. He made a mental note to fix it with a huge discount. Selena was a beauty that Frank had every intention of having fun with. Married or not, he was going to get in her good graces and her panties. Strolling to his truck that was parked directly in front of the entrance, Frank got in and led the way to the restaurant.

Frank had known Hayden for years and he always serviced the businessman's vehicles. When Hayden brought his Porsche into the shop, he kind of told Frank about the incident and what happened at the bar with Selena's husband. Selena could pretend she was happily married, but Frank knew that was far from the truth. In a matter of time, he would see just how dedicated she was to her cheating-ass husband.

Pulling into an empty spot outside of a popular soul food restaurant, Frank exited his truck as he waited for Selena to get out of her vehicle. Escorting her inside, Frank and Selena placed their orders and talked about everything under the sun. They laughed, joked, and just enjoyed lunch while getting to know each other on a friendly level.

It had been a while since Selena had actually enjoyed a day out without thinking about the turmoil of her marriage and crying her eyes out. She saw the lunch date as a way of getting away from her reality, and she really needed it. Frank, on the other hand, listened to Selena talk about herself, her likes and dislikes, and also on being a mother. He paid close attention, but never indulged anything about himself other than how he started his business.

Frank had a wife that was in the Army. She had been deployed for the past year and he didn't know when she was coming home. In the meantime, he was lonely and in need of a temporary female companion. He'd had his share of sexual partners, but they all ended because the woman wanted more than he could give. Selena came around at the right time because the two of them could take all the stress out of each other's lives for the time being with no strings attached.

Meesha

Chapter 5

Samir was sent home under investigation for the allegations Lavita blurted out about their work relationship. Mr. Whittaker also said he wanted to go back and look at the footage to see if Samir was anywhere near when Lavita was stealing from the accounts. Even though Samir swore he didn't have anything to do with her criminal activities, his word wasn't good enough for his boss. They were looking at his finances as well, and that pissed him off even more. Samir was grateful for the fact they were not freezing his accounts while they investigated.

Sitting in his living room with a much-needed wood filled with the finest weed, Samir just sat thinking about his next move. He'd called Selena on several occasions and she hadn't answered one of them. There was no reason to blow her line up because it would've only angered her more than she already was. After all that transpired at his job, he reached out to Chade for advice. Chade was busy at the time and promised to stop by before he headed home.

While waiting for the time to pass, Samir went into the kitchen to prep his dinner. He had a taste for lasagna and planned to throw together one with lots of spinach, mushrooms, and onions. The dish was something he and Selena would prepare together, and Samir experienced a wave of unhappiness doing the deed alone. It was too quiet in the house, so he walked back into the living room and grabbed the remote for the surround sound speaker. Finding his favorite playlist on his phone, Samir just hit play and walked away. "Someone you Loved" by Lewis Capaldi flowed through the room.

Samir shook his head because the song said everything he was thinking about Selena as a person. She was the person that knew him inside out. To have that one person he could rely on and loved him unconditionally at a point, just walk away as if what they had meant nothing tugged at his heart. His wife was his escape through many things. and he felt she turned her back on him without even letting him apologize for his fuck-up. Samir knew what he'd done shouldn't have ever happened, but it did, and he regretted it every day.

I'm going under, and this time, I fear there's no one to turn to
This all or nothing way of loving got me sleeping without you
Now, I need somebody to know, somebody to hear
Somebody to have, just to know how it feels
It's easy to say, but it's never the same
Guess I like the way you help me escape

Now the day bleeds into nightfall
And you're not here to get me through it all
I let my guard down and then you pulled the rug
I was getting kind of used to being someone you loved

Actually, listening to the lyrics to the song, Samir felt he was being selfish because he had no right to think about having his wife in his presence to love when he was the one that had done the unthinkable act. As he prepared the veggie pie, thoughts of Selena and their situation invaded his mind, causing Samir to pick up his phone to call her again. The results were the same. Instead of hanging up, Samir waited for the prompt to leave a message.

"Selena, I know you don't want to have anything to do with me right now, but I want you to know I'm terribly sorry for causing so much pain in your life. You have every right to feel the way you do and I'll give you all the time in the world to do whatever you deem fit. I love you, babe. Give me a call so we can talk openly and work on moving forward."

Samir placed his phone on the counter and went to work on his dinner. Dicing vegetables and singing along with the music that kept him company, he finally layered the pie, adding chicken breast at the last minute before shoving it in the oven. He prepared a salad along with garlic bread before going to take a quick shower before Chade was set to arrive.

As the water cascaded down his body, Samir thought about how his life went from sugar to shit in a matter of months. Lavita was a mistake he wished he'd never ventured off with. Not only did he lose his family, but now his job was in jeopardy. For six years he'd loved on Selena and envisioned their happily ever after. The two of them were destined to grow old together. Samir messed it up by not addressing the elephant that sat comfortably in their home during a time which should've brought them closer together. Instead, a wedge was placed in the center of the love they had built.

While pulling on a long-sleeved shirt with a pair of joggers, Samir slipped his feet into his slides and made his way back to the kitchen. The lasagna smelled good and was almost ready for him to devour. Looking at the clock, it was almost five o'clock and the day had dwindled away. Being home when he should've been at work was something Samir wasn't used to and had no plans of becoming accustomed to doing. He sat at the table and pulled his laptop from his briefcase to search for jobs in case he was let go.

Samir stomach growled in anticipation of the dinner he would be pigging out on. His phone rang and he got up to get it from the counter. Hoping it was Selena, he glanced at the screen and saw it was his mother on the other end. Sitting back at the table, he answered the call.

"Hey, beautiful. How you doing?" Samir sang.

"Don't hey beautiful me! Where is my granddaughter, Samir?"

Here we go with this bullshit, Samir said to himself after what his mother said. Gloria Jamison was always calling trying to play mediator in Samir's marriage. Little did she know, Selena was the one that didn't want anything to do with her son.

"Sevyn is with her mother. You probably should've called Selena about that because I only see her on selective days."

"You wouldn't have that problem if you hadn't messed around with a no-good-ass woman. Tell me what this hussy got to offer that made you go against the grain. And don't say pussy because your wife has one of those too, you know."

"Ma, why would I say something like that to you? That's so disrespectful. To answer your question, I wasn't looking for anything other than that, to be honest. I didn't see myself going any further than the bedroom with her."

"In other words, she's a hood rat that stays in the gutter and just so happened to work with you. Is that what you're telling me?"

49

"Come on, Ma. Go on with that crap. I don't know anything about that girl, okay?"

His mother was quiet for a spell before she went in on Samir again. "You didn't learn the formalities about *that girl*, but you thought it was alright to cheat on your wife with her. Sounds ass backwards to me because she could've been having sex with every Tom, Dick, and Harry while you were laying down with her. That's what's wrong with you young folks today. Y'all don't think before you fuck! Now look at'cha, walking around with a long-ass chin because you lost the best thing to ever give a damn about your black ass!"

If Samir didn't already feel like shit for what he'd done, with his mother coming down on him, it only made him feel even worse than he already felt. For her to come at him with all the rah-rah only let Samir know she'd talked to Selena at some point in time about the situation.

"Ma, it wasn't like that at all. Before you attack me, did you think about the way Selena pushed me away? She never wanted me to touch her before and after Sevyn was born. What was I supposed to do?"

"Beat yo' meat until she decided to give you the pleasure you were seeking! That was the time for you to love her better than you've ever loved her before. Not go elsewhere." Sandra was giving it to her son the hard way. "Being pregnant with all types of body changes and mood swings isn't easy, son. If men knew what the hell women went through during that time, y'all wouldn't be quick to drop babies off in the womb."

"I'm not in the mood to talk about this anymore, Ma. I've already been deemed the bad guy and I'm eating it. I have more trying things to concentrate on. I'll talk to you later," Samir said as the doorbell chimed.

"Okay, this conversation isn't over. I want to see Sevyn, Samir."

"Call Selena and let her know you want to spend time with the baby. She's not answering any of my calls right now. I just took Sevyn back to her this morning, and don't ask why I didn't come over. I needed to spend time with my daughter alone," Samir said, walking to the door, snatching it open. "I gotta go, Ma. Chade is here. I love you."

"I love you too. We can talk more about this tomorrow when I come to your job. Lunch on me."

Samir sighed. "I'm not working tomorrow, but I'll come over so we can sit and talk about everything, okay?"

"That sounds like a plan. Talk to you later."

Finally, being able to get his mother off the phone was a relief for Samir. She could always sense when something was bothering him and she knew it went beyond his marital issues. He had to mentally prepare himself for the lunch date because he was going to lay everything on the table when he came clean with his mother. The backlash she was going to dish out was something he would have to suck up and take without any rebuttal.

Chade was sitting at the table when Samir entered the dining room. He went straight to the kitchen to remove the lasagna from the oven and placed it on the stovetop to cool. Placing the garlic bread in the oven to toast, he sat across from his friend with the most pitiful look on his face.

"Don't look so down, man. Troubles don't last always. Do you have any Heineken in the fridge? I need to prepare myself for whatever you're about to talk about."

Samir nodded his head and got up to get the beers. He glanced over his shoulder as he bent down, "I hope you told Baylei you wouldn't be home for dinner. This may take a while, and I apologize in advance for calling you over on such short notice."

"You don't have to apologize for shit. This what we do, nigga. I know you'd do the same for me if the shoe was on the other foot. You gon' have to share that damn food though. I haven't eaten since lunch and I'm hungry as hell."

"That ain't nothing. I made more than enough lasagna and you're welcome to take some with you too. We can talk while enjoying my delectable entrée." Samir smirked.

Chade laughed at his friend's choice of words because Samir sounded like a rich-ass butler. Samir went to take the bread out and fixed both of them a plate. By the time Samir set the plates on the table, Chade had washed his hands, taken off his suit jacket, and rolled up the sleeves on his button down.

"So, what's up? I heard you tell your ma that Selena was still rejecting your calls." Chade drank from the bottle of beer before picking up his fork to dig into the cheesy pie.

"Yeah, you heard right, but that's not what I want to talk about," Samir said, following suit by sipping his beer. "I was sent home from work today. I'm actually on suspension," he said, shaking his head.

Chade's eyes bucked because there wasn't a day that went by when Samir wasn't busting his ass at his job. The man had all types of certificates and awards for his hard work hanging in his office. To hear that he was suspended was surprising to hear. He was a great financial advisor and he was good at what he did for a living. Samir pushed his plate to the middle of the table and folded his hands in front of him then continued his story.

"The FBI was there when I arrived this morning, along with my boss. Do you remember me telling y'all Lavita was under investigation?" Chade nodded his head because his mouth was full. "Well, they know a lot more about the extracurricular activities she's been indulging in at the bank. Man, Lavita stole a quarter mil from them."

"Damn, she was hittin' they ass hard!" Chade exclaimed. "I hope she's living large around these parts with that type of bread."

Samir knew Lavita wasn't living a lavish life because he'd driven to her apartment multiple times to pick her up for their rendezvous. She still drove the same 2003 Chevy Tahoe and runover flats she wore to her interview. Hell, Lavita was bringing bag lunch to work every day as if going out for lunch wasn't in her budget. Unlike many women that worked with him, Samir noticed Lavita only got her hair done maybe twice every other month. Any other time, it was in a bun on top of her head. There was no way anyone would've known she was sitting on so much money.

"Nah. Lavita lives in the projects in Compton. That's why I was surprised when they revealed the three hundred fifty thousand dollars she had stolen."

"What did she have to say when they threw their findings at her?" Chade asked.

"At first, she tried to say someone else made the transactions under her ID number. They weren't buying that story because they had video off her in action." Samir laughed. "There wasn't shit Lavita could say to get out of that jam. Her face was in the camera clear as day. On top of it all, the dude she had to help her is sitting in custody, probably with a lesser sentence because he told on her ass."

Chade was laughing as he thought about a time he saw a similar situation unfold in front of him when he first started working in banking. Folks would lie to the Pope to get out of a jam they put themselves in, not realizing there's cameras all over any bank they stepped foot in. Hell, the cameras are trained on the tellers more than the clients that come through the glass doors. How stupid could one be?

"Look, I highly doubt you had anything to do with that conspiracy. It's messed up that you're in this predicament, to be honest. They have nothing on you because if they did, they would've walked you out in cuffs too."

"I'm not worried about that. I was suspended because the bitch told them about us messing around. Put my ass right in the spotlight, man."

"That's small shit to a giant, Samir. They could only get you on fraternizing on the job. Don't get me wrong, they are going to go over those tapes with a fine-tooth comb to make sure you had nothing to do with the underhanded shit Lavita did, but if you didn't do shit, then that's all they got. You may lose your job though. It's not the end of the world because you can get another one. In fact, just tell me when you get the call. I'll hire you on with me on the spot."

Chade was a real one. He would never allow his homeboy to be without a job if he could help it. Knowing Chade had his back in the midst of his fuck up eased Samir's mind drastically. Money wasn't an issue. It was the simple fact of sitting around worrying about losing his family on top of work to occupy his time.

"Thanks for having my back. Getting another job wouldn't be a problem. It's not having shit to do while thinking about Selena that bothers me."

"What's going on with that?" Chade asked as he sat back in the chair.

"She's still talking divorce, unfortunately. I've been beating her phone down since I dropped Sevyn off this morning. The stubborn side of my wife is in full effect because she refuses to answer." Samir ran his hand down his face, looking straight ahead at nothing in particular.

"I was ready to body that nigga. When I saw him gazing in Selena's eyes, something inside my body clicked. Knowing we're going through all this turmoil because I fucked around with someone that wasn't worth a damn had me kicking myself every time I thought about what I'd done."

"Yeah, before they said anything about Selena hitting his ride, I just knew shit was about to go left. It's not worth fighting over though. If Selena is adamant about calling it quits, you have to let it go. Like I told you before, give her space and co-parent for the time being," Chade said, standing to his feet. He stretched and rubbed his belly as he let out a loud, boisterous belch.

"Damn, nigga, you good?" Samir laughed.

"You put your foot in that lasagna. Thanks for dinner, fam, but I gotta go home to my wife. Keep me posted about your job. I got you, Samir," Chade said, reaching for his empty plate.

Samir nodded his head. "Leave that there, I got it. Thank you for always being there for me, bro." He walked around and gave his friend a brotherly hug before walking into the kitchen. He brought back two wrapped plates and handed them to Chade. "Make sure my sis gets her plate too."

"I'll have to see about that. I may just hide both of them in the fridge because I don't think I can share this." Chade laughed.

"Get out!"

Chade and Samir joked around for a few minutes more before Samir closed the door locking it behind his friend. Turning to go back to the kitchen, reality set in and the silence around him damn near stopped him from breathing. Having someone else in the presence of his home felt like everything to Samir, and it was gone the instant Chade departed. He had to find a way to prove to his wife how sorry he was before depression set in too deep.

Meesha

Chapter 6

Selena sat up the majority of the night looking for a lawyer to represent her in the divorce process. As she researched on the internet, Selena hoped Samir wouldn't fight her on her decision of divorce because he was the reason she had to go the route she was going. The only thing she was looking for from him was support for his daughter which Selena knew was not going to be the problem in the entire process.

Being a professional photographer brought in lots of money for Selena and she never needed her husband financially. Samir made good money working at the bank and Selena had no problem playing her part as the wife and allowing her husband to be the man of the house. Samir took care of all the bills and Selena took care of everything else around the house. She cooked, cleaned, bought all the toiletries, and anything she and her husband needed, including his underwear and socks.

There were never any rough patches in their relationship up until the point of Samir's infidelity; at least none that ever got back to Selena. In her mind, she had the perfect life. Hell, Samir was the perfect husband any woman would ever want to claim as their own. From the spontaneous date nights to the surprise gifts and attentive way he loved her, Selena had no complaints. Now she couldn't stomach seeing his name appear on her phone every hour on the hour.

After writing down the information for the attorney she'd found, Selena went into the bathroom to take care of her hygiene. She was going to call the attorney and get the ball rolling on the divorce. There was no use waiting it out. Selena's decision was final and her marriage to Samir was truly over.

The lunch outing with Frank played in her mind and she smiled. The two of them actually had a good time the day they went out for lunch. They walked around enjoying the weather because neither of them was ready to go their separate ways. Selena could see a great friendship blooming between them, but it wouldn't go any further than that. When she realized it was well into the evening, she and Frank exchanged numbers. He even set a date to fix her car for a low rate.

After six years of being with the same man, it was time for Selena to learn how to love herself. Being alone might open her mind to new things and give her the opportunity to concentrate on her business along with Sevyn. Samir had broken her heart one too many times, and there was no coming back from it.

The sound of Sevyn crying brought Selena out of the thoughts she was having and she scrambled back into the bedroom. Dressed in a pink onesie that read "Daddy's girl", Selena smiled at the little replica of Samir lying in her bassinet fussing while kicking her little feet. Missing the times when she would've been able to get right in the shower because Samir would've beaten her to the baby, Selena shook the thought and reached down, picking up her little bundle.

"What's wrong with that baby?" she asked, rocking Sevyn in her arms.

Settling down for a few seconds, her daughter sucked on her fist and wailed loudly. Selena knew exactly what was wrong and reached for the bottle she'd premade. Taking a seat on the side of the bed, Sevyn quieted down soon as she saw the bottle full of milk. As she looked at her daughter, "Ordinary Love" by Sade disrupted her mommy/daughter time. Selena didn't have to look to see who was calling because there was only one person in her phone with a customized ringtone, and that was her husband.

"Good morning, Samir."

"Good morning to you too, Selena. Sorry to call so early. This is about the time Sevyn would want her breakfast. I was calling to make sure she was getting what her heart desires."

Selena ended the call without saying anything and dialed Samir right back with the camera trained on their daughter. Samir answered and talked to his daughter throughout her feeding. One thing Selena couldn't take away from him was the love he gave their daughter. Sevyn stopped sucking on the milk every so often and smiled at Samir as she kept her eyes on the image before her.

"What's your plans for the day?" Samir asked.

"I have some business to take care of. Why?"

"What time? Because I can come get Sevyn while you're out. I don't want your mother to think she has to care for my daughter all the time."

"Samir, I'm still on maternity leave for another week. I'm here majority of the time with her. You don't have to make excuses to come get Sevyn. Shouldn't you be getting ready for work?"

"I took some time off," he lied.

"Oh. In that case, if you want her for the day, I don't have a problem with that at all. I'll have her ready for you.

"Thank you. Hit me up when you're ready for me to come."

"Samir, you don't have to thank me. Sevyn has nothing to do with what we have going on. I don't answer when you call all the time because every time you call isn't about our daughter. The last thing I want to discuss with you is the situation. It's final, and I'm going to file for divorce. You can come whenever. She'll be ready."

Selena ended the call and placed the phone on the bed. After burping Sevyn, she walked into the bathroom and turned the water off in the shower. Getting her daughter ready for Samir was her priority because she didn't want him standing over her when he arrived. All Selena wanted was to hand their daughter over and watch Samir walk back out the door.

She chose a cute purple sweatsuit for Sevyn to wear with a pair of purple and white Chucks. Her daughter was too beautiful and had fallen asleep while Selena got her ready for the day with her father. As she packed the diaper bag with diapers, wipes, milk, and a couple outfits, the sound of the doorbell grabbed Selena's attention. Quickly throwing a few other items in the bag, Selena zipped it up and placed it on the bed. Turning around, she came face to face with her soon-to-be ex-husband.

Samir looked good as hell in the black Balenciaga sweatsuit and matching sneakers. The hair on his face wasn't neatly trimmed and was kind of scruffy, but it didn't take from his appearance. Forcing her eyes away from him, Selena went back to attending to the baby.

"I just have to get her blanket and she will be ready to go," Selena said without looking up.

"Selena, do you really plan on filing for divorce?" Samir sat on the edge of the bed while waiting for his wife to answer the question he'd asked. When she continued fumbling around the room, he opened his mouth to speak once again, but Selena took that moment to speak.

"I have a little time, so we can talk this through like adults. Samir, I want to apologize for allowing months to go by without addressing our situation. Six years together and I gave my all and never looked in the direction of another man with any type of desire. For years, we talked about starting a family. Both of us were so happy to finally see a positive result on the pregnancy test then you go out and sleep with someone else while I suffered through depression."

"Selena, I—"

"I'm not finished, Samir," Selena said, cutting him off before he could continue. "During my pregnancy, I know I was hard to deal with. I tried my best to shake the negative thoughts out of my mind. Being pregnant, going through the changes my body was experiencing right before my eyes, had me feeling ugly and undesirable." Tears welled in Selena's eyes as she turned away from Samir's gaze.

"When I received the picture of you and your side bitch, I was hesitant to mention it to you because I had enough of my own shit to deal with. You started moving around me as if we were roommates. I understand you were trying to console me on many occasions, but I didn't want to be touched. The change in you made me angry causing my mind to wander back to you spending time with another woman. After I asked you about the picture, you lied to my face."

Samir stared sadly at his wife because hearing her say she felt ugly and undesirable had him feeling some type of way. He thought about the times he tried to comfort her by rubbing her feet, stomach, and anything else he could while Selena pushed him away at every turn. There was nothing he could say or do about lying because he had already done the deed.

"Selena, I did everything to make you see I was all in with you during the pregnancy. You never told me anything about the feelings you were having. Instead, you pushed me to the side, and I let you have that. Trying to appease you the best way I could wasn't working. I apologize once again for my actions. You have shown me nothing but love throughout our entire relationship, and I'm grateful. Thank you for loving me. I've loved you the entire time as well, whether you believe me or not. Lavita didn't mean anything to me, and I regret dealing with her."

So, she has a name, Selena thought, rolling her eyes.

"My mama handed my ass to me last night. She and Malik explained some things to me, and I understand now. When everything was going on, I took it as you not wanting to be bothered and I left it alone, as you requested. Knowing what I know today, I should've sat down and forced you to bare your soul about how you were really feeling at the time."

Everything Samir said went in one ear and out the other. Selena didn't really care at that point. She did have a few questions that needed to be answered. Hopefully, Samir would be man enough to lay it on the table truthfully. Sevyn fussed and Samir reached over to place the binky in her mouth to settle her down. After their daughter dozed off to sleep, Selena sat next to her husband with her hands clamped together.

"Talk to me, Selena. Get it all off your chest now. There's no reason to hold everything that's on your mind inside."

"How long were you involved with this woman, Samir?"

He didn't have anything to lose. His family was a thing of the past, and he didn't see any reason to lie about anything else. "I slept with Lavita from time to time for at least six months. We went out and did other things outside of fucking so no, that wasn't all we were doing. Lavita gave me the attention you stopped providing at home. Was it right for me to seek that outside of our marriage? No, but it happened. I can't change the past, Selena. What I really want is for you to think about counseling before making a drastic move and going straight for divorce. We can work through this, and I promise, I will never step out on our union ever again. Lavita and I are over. I cut all ties with her because my family is more important than anything."

"I've heard enough, and my decision stands. If you cheated once, you would cheat again. The thing about all of this is, I won't sit back and wait for it to happen a second time. I'm going to be honest; I will never be able to trust you, Samir. You give off all the vibes of my daddy. I refuse to become my mama."

"Selena, I'm nothing like your father. Yes, I cheated on you, but I'm not trying to leave you and my daughter to be with another woman. What I did was a mistake. I've owned up to the shit and want to make it right. Dissolving our union without working on things is a huge mistake in my opinion. All I ask is that you go to counseling with me. Can you do that?" Samir held his breath, waiting for his wife's response. She sat shaking her head no without giving any thought to what he'd suggested.

"I can go to counseling, but I'm not. What's the point of fighting for something that has been tarnished because of you? If I forgive you for the shit you have done, that will give you the green light to do it again. I'm not about to turn into a detective when my degree is Fine Arts in Photography. I'm going to file the paperwork, and it should be relatively easy for both of us. The only thing I want out of the proceedings is for you to be the best father you can be to Sevyn. I don't want anything from you. I'll find a place to live and purchase another car. You can keep any and everything you have ever bought for me. I can get the material shit again, but I won't be able to regain my peace or keep my sanity. It's not worth going back and forth in court because we still have to be cordial with one another in order to co-parent."

Hearing Selena say she didn't even want to work things out deflated Samir's chest. "If that's how you want to do this, I must honor it. As far as you returning the car, leaving your belongings, and finding a place, you don't have to do any of that. I will move out and you and Sevyn can stay at the house. You didn't have to mention me taking care of our daughter because that's a given. I would never turn my back on her. To make it easier for you, I'll go down and file for child support myself."

Selena got up and went to her closet, pulling out her outfit for the day. She laid out a pair of black leggings with a long-sleeved black t-shirt on the bed before responding to Samir. "You do what you feel is best. I'm going to do what's best for me. I have things to do, so I have to take a shower and get my day going."

Samir took that as his cue to gather Sevyn and her belongings to head out. He wanted so badly to ask where she was going, but it wasn't his place to question her. Samir had to take the situation as it was and give Selena what she wanted, and that was getting out of the marriage. He'd tried his best to reconcile with her, and she wasn't trying to hear anything other than divorce. The only thing Samir could do was wait for the papers to arrive and sign off on them. It wasn't going to change how he felt about Selena and their child. Samir was prepared to do whatever, and that included taking care of his family from afar.

Meesha

Chapter 7

"Aye, Sanji! What's for dinner?"

Sanji was chilling at the firehouse and as usual, he was expected to cook for the entire crew. *What the hell I look like, Chef Boyardee?* Sanji thought as he closed his eyes lying on his bunk. Hearing his door creak open, Sanji didn't bother looking to see who had entered because he wanted whoever it was to respect the fact that he was sleeping. They didn't.

He felt a hand running through his locs and jumped up, pushing the person to the floor. What he didn't do was play that man-on-man shit, and Sanji was ready to slap a muthafucka for invading his personal space. Sanji realized he'd pushed one of the female firefighters away from him.

"Ciana, what are you doing in here?" Sanji asked coolly.

"Josh sent me to ask if you're cooking tonight. You looked so peaceful and handsome. I couldn't resist reaching out to touch something."

Ciana was new to the firehouse and had been riding Sanji's dick from day one. It seemed the more he rejected her, the harder she came at him. His resistance was wearing down. The thought of having Jordyn at home was the only thing saving the beauty standing before him from getting bent over to receive what she was looking for.

Sanji couldn't ignore the fact that Ciana was stacked from her voluptuous hips to her perky breasts. Her stomach was flat with a four pack that was sculpted to perfection. Sanji thought about running his tongue over each one of her pecks and spreading her thighs wide until he reached her creamy center, but he had to stay away from her because there was nothing but trouble waiting on the other side. Crossing the thin line was something Sanji would only fantasize about.

"Tell Josh to go out and buy whatever he wants cooked. I'm not cooking and footing the bill. For the record, I've told you this time and time again; I have a woman that I love at home. There will be nothing going on between you and me. That would lead to complications I don't need in my life. Now, if I was single, we could get it on and poppin'." Sanji smirked.

"What your girl have to do with me? What happens in the house, stays in the house. It's up to you if you get in the pussy and forget all you have going on in the real world. That's on you."

"To answer your question, my woman has nothing to do with you. There will be no foul play on my part because I respect what I have going on in my life. I can tell you right now, if I drop this dick off in you, I won't be the one running around dizzy. Now, move around and go tell Josh what I said."

Being on the job for twenty-four hours every other day for five days kept Sanji away from Jordyn more than he wanted to be, but the four consecutive days he had off made up for the time spent at the firehouse. Jordyn always made sure he was well-fed and sexually satisfied before he left to go back to work. The days she brought him sweet little nothings, or just to show him love, were highlights of his day. They would talk, text, and Facetime whenever they could, and the love was growing between the two.

Sanji watched Ciana strut from the room with her ass singing one cheek, two cheek, as he silently counted the jiggles in his head. Glancing up at the clock on the wall, he saw that it was only three o'clock in the afternoon, and he wanted the night to be over sooner than later. Sanji couldn't wait to sleep with Jordyn pressed against his chest while her ass soothed the ache in his wood. Thinking about his better half, his phone rang, causing a smile to graced his lips as he saw Jordyn's beautiful face on display.

"Good afternoon, Beautiful. How did your day at work go for you?" Sanji asked, lying back on his bunk.

"It's been tiring. Baylei is working me to the bone, but I wouldn't trade my position for anything in the world." Sanji could hear the smile in her voice which caused him to smile as well. "I was calling because I miss you, first and foremost. Also, to inform you that I will be going out to dinner with the girls."

"Baby, you don't have to tell me your every move. I trust you enough to know you will be on your best behavior while out of my sight. You are mine and forever will belong to me and only me. Enjoy yourself, love."

Jordyn was quiet because as of late, she had been experiences dreams about her late ex and felt guilty for moving on with Sanji. She and Lamar had plans of living happily ever after before his untimely death. In her dreams, Lamar was trying to tell Jordyn something, but before he could do so, she would wake up in a sweat, crying herself back to sleep. The weird part about it was the fact that she only experienced the dreams when Sanji was at work overnight. Jordyn hadn't spoken to anyone about the things she was going through, and it was the sole reason she asked her girls to meet for a girl's night on a Monday.

"Aye, what are you thinking about over there?" Sanji asked.

"Oh, I'm sorry. I was going over a client's file and I zoned out for a minute. I will enjoy myself, Sanji. It's always a happy moment with my sisters. How's things going there? It seems quiet today."

"Every time you say that, we get a call to go out and fight some type of fire or rushing out to an accident." Sanji laughed. "You are correct though; it has been quiet thus far. These folks have appointed me as the fire cook of Engine 98. That's what I'll be doing once Josh returns with the ingredients to whatever he has a taste for."

The light in the hall vanished, forcing Sanji to turn his attention toward the door. Ciana stood lusting over him with her hand in her mouth. Shaking his head, Sanji focused on the conversation he was having with Jordyn as he ignored the enticing gesture Ciana was throwing in his direction. Jordyn was talking about his expertise cooking skills when Ciana's voice interrupted their them.

"Josh is back with the food. Are you ready to eat?" she smirked. "I mean are you ready to cook?"

"Who is that?" Jordyn asked, concentrating on the background noise in the firehouse.

Sanji stared at Ciana as if she was some type of plague. It wasn't a secret to anyone at the workplace that Sanji had a woman, but Ciana tried to get his attention at every turn, and he'd curbed her each time. His thoughts went wild at times and in his defense, he'd never acted on them. At that point, Sanji knew her chances of rolling around in the hay with him would forever be a dream because she would be trouble in the making if gave her what she was looking for.

"Ciana, don't play with me. I'm a grown-ass man and my livelihood is something I don't fuck with like that on any level. Make that your last time disrespecting my woman and me in that manner. Don't ever come back to my room, or we will have more problems than you could ever deal with. If it's not about business, don't utter a word to me."

Ciana sauntered away with a smile on her face which only made Sanji madder than he already was. Once she disappeared down the hall, he gave Jordyn his undivided attention. He knew there was no way to sugarcoat what had just happened and the time to address it was at that point.

"That was nothing. To be honest with you, she is a firefighter that works here and yes, she has been coming on strong to me. Jordyn, there's nothing going on with me and her, so please don't think too much into it. I checked the shit and it will be the last time I'll have to say anything else to her about it."

"I doubt that, but I'm going to allow you to handle it any way you see fit. I'm a woman before anything, Sanji, and I know from past experiences, she's going to be a problem. It's up to you to keep her out of your face because if I walk up on it, I can't promise to be on my best behavior. I trust you until there's reason for me not to."

"Indeed. Don't let this take your mind to a negative place. I'm content with what we have, Jordyn. No other female will ever be able to break us. Get back to work, enjoy the rest of your day, and have fun with your girls. I'll see you in the morning, baby."

"Talk to you later," Jordyn replied, before ending the call.

Sanji could feel the lack of energy at the end of the conversation with Jordyn. What Ciana did was disrespectful. Sanji knew he had to address the shit further because if he didn't make sure his point was heard, Ciana would continue with her silly antics. Standing from his bunk, Sanji clipped his phone on his hip while walking to the kitchen.

"He's in there on the phone with his girl," Ciana could be heard saying with a hint of humor in her voice. "I'm going to get my hands on him and he's gonna forget all about Little Miss Sunshine. It's only a matter of time before Sanji realize the phatty I'm packing holds more heat than the mediocre shit he rushes home to when he's off the clock."

Ciana didn't realize all the laughter ceased around her. With her back turned away from the entryway, she had no clue Sanji was propped against the door jamb with his arms folded over his chest. Josh looked up and opened his mouth to speak, but the shake of Sanji's head put a halt to it.

"I mean, look at me. What man do y'all know would turn a Puerto Rican mami like myself down? Not only do I have a career with my own money, unlike his bitch, I don't need him to take care of me. I'm down to build with his ass and collaborate to make beautiful babies together."

Ciana was doing the very thing he came to talk to her about; still disrespecting. Walking in on her rant only pissed Sanji off more because she was sharing it with the entire house. Noticing no one was giving any feedback to her foolishness, Ciana turned slowly towards the door and her eyes bulged out of the sockets. She got up and proceeded in Sanji's direction, but he held up his hand, halting her steps.

"It would be best for you to stay the fuck away from me. I've already told you to stop with the bullshit you trying to be on. I may be the sergeant in this house and carry myself in a professional manner, but if you want to go another route and see my bad side, keep playing in my face."

Ciana smirked, "You know you want me, Sergeant Kaneko. Stop putting on for others and give in to your wants. See, you need a woman that can help you build, not a woman that needs you to take care of her."

Sanji was fuming from the inside out listening to Ciana talk about things she really knew nothing about. At that point, he knew she was going to be a major problem to his career and his relationship with Jordyn. There was no way he would allow a woman to take anything of importance away from him.

"I will report your ass for sexual harassment if you keep talking out the side of your neck. Many men wouldn't even think on the same level as myself, but before you attempt to get me, I'm already two steps ahead."

Sanji walked across the room and sat down on an empty stool. Josh kept cutting up vegetables with his back turned as he listened to the back and forth between the two. He agreed with Sanji one hundred percent, and Ciana was dead wrong for how she was approaching him.

"Ciana, Sarge is right. You have to lay off the flirting because he isn't interested in dealing with you on that level. Pushing up on him is only going to cause tension in the house, and we don't need all of that madness. I can tell you this, it won't work in your favor. I can see this being the downfall of your career."

"What's wrong with two consensual adults having a little fun outside of work?" Ciana asked.

"That's the problem, young lady. Sanji isn't trying to have fun with you. He has a woman at home. I've heard him fighting you off on many occasions, and you keep coming back," Bill, an older guy, said. "I've been on this job many years, and mixing business with pleasure doesn't always work out. You need to learn to let things go. If Sarge reports this as harassment, he would have every right to do so."

Ciana eyes turned to slits. She was angry because the same men voicing their thoughts were the same men laughing as she talked about Sanji when he wasn't around. Ciana wasn't used to any man turning her down under any circumstance, and it didn't sit well with her. Being one of two women in the firehouse, she was outnumbered with the men.

"In order for any of this shit to have merit, *Sarge* would need proof of harassment. Which he doesn't have." Ciana laughed. "I'm going to wait for you to put that dick in my life, Kaneko. You're going to love it here."

Bridgette, the other female in the house, had heard enough. She rose up from her seat and stalked across the room grabbing Ciana's arm. "Let me holla at you, sis." Trying to free her arm out of the grip Bridgette had on her, Ciana failed miserably. "Now!"

Watching as the two women left out of the kitchen area, Sanji let out a heavy sigh. He ran a hand down his face while shaking his head. Stopping the recording on his phone, Sanji laid the device on the counter.

"You recorded all of that?" Joey asked with a smile.

"Damn right I did. Ciana is wicked with her shit, and I refuse to get caught in a jam behind her thirsty ass. When she disrespected Jordyn earlier, I knew I had to move differently around her. One thing I refuse to do is come to work walking on eggshells because she doesn't know what the fuck no means. It took hard work and dedication to get where I am. Pussy won't be the thing to snatch it all away."

"I feel you on that," Josh said, wiping his hands on a paper towel. "Enough about all that. Get over here and do what you do best. I'm hungry as hell."

Sanji washed his hands and went to work on the chili Josh wanted so badly. Being a white boy, Josh always wanted Sanji to cook soulful dinners, and he loved every morsel. He wasn't the only one either. The entire house stayed ready to eat whenever Sanji graced the kitchen with his skills.

"I got y'all. Get ready to call home about that unseasoned shit y'all used to eating on your off days." Sanji laughed as he put his foot in the food he was preparing.

Meesha

Chapter 8

Toni sat waiting for Jordyn and Baylei to arrive at The Palm, which was an upscale restaurant in Downtown L.A. Toni had been wanting to come to the restaurant for some time since she read all the great reviews it. She was glad she didn't have to go home and change, because the atmosphere didn't call for casual clothing. As she sipped on the white wine she'd ordered, Toni thought about all the love Malik had been showing her over the past few months.

Her mental mindset was still a little foggy after the death of her cousin, but she was pushing through every day. Going to therapy helped her in so many ways because getting through the tragedy she endured by herself was something she couldn't handle on her own. Many black people were against going to therapy, and Toni was one of them, but she knew outside help was her best option when she felt herself diving into the black hole she saw herself getting sucked into.

Having a strong man standing beside her was a plus. Malik not only told Toni he loved her every day; he went over and beyond to show it. His family embraced and welcomed her into their home with opened arms. It was a huge surprise for Toni to walk into her paralegal firm and see everything her man had done.

"Hey, chica!" Baylei squealed, approaching the table.

A few heads turned in their direction, but the friends didn't care. With their busy schedules, they hadn't seen one another since Toni's grand opening. Baylei had a glow that made her facial features pop more than Toni had ever seen. Chade had brought out so much in her friend in such a short time. Baylei was never that happy when she was with Noah. She couldn't be herself then, but now, she was a free spirit.

"Damn, I can't get no love," Jordyn sassed as she walked up.

"Shut up and get over here! I've missed you too, sissy. It's been too long since we've hung out. These damn men got us neglecting one another." Toni rolled her eyes as she embraced Jordyn.

"Don't speak for me, bitch," Baylei scoffed. "Chade hasn't kept me away from no damn body. Now my job is another story. When

I accepted the position to run Wes' company here, it was supposed to be easy breezy. However, the architect bug that I possessed early on just won't let me be great. I just have to be hands-on with every project waiting in the queue."

Jordyn smacked her lips as she took a sip of wine. "You overwork yourself when you don't have to, Lei. The architects you oversee are great at what they do. I've heard Wes tell you on many occasions to allow them to do the work they are getting paid to do. Hell, if I was in a position to sit back and look cute, I would run with that shit."

"Of course, you would, and that's why you are just my assistant." Baylei laughed. "I can't sit back and do nothing. I like to be in on the buzz. The only reason you want me to lay off so much work is because you want to be able to kick your feet up in the corner office I put you in. I hate to be the bearer of bad news, Jordyn, but you, too, will work for your hefty salary. Nothing in Lei's world come for free. Sister or no sister, you gon' put in work."

"Enough about all that. What's been going on in y'all lives?" Toni asked.

"I've just been working and going home at night." Jordyn hunched her shoulders. "I'm basically at home alone since Sanji spends majority of his time at the damn firehouse. If it wasn't for Miss Margie, I would've been gone crazy."

"What do you mean, Jordyn?" Baylei asked with concern.

Biting her bottom lip, Jordyn placed her head in the palm of her hands. "I've been having dreams about Lamar again, but these are different from the other ones."

Jordyn started having dreams about her late ex the night after his death. At first, Lamar would just appear in her dreams smiling at her. It calmed her soul and allowed her to sleep peacefully. Lamar's passing hurt Jordyn because he was the love of her life. They were together from their freshman year at Kenwood High School. The two were inseparable, and there wasn't a moment one was seen without the other. Jordyn and Lamar had that undeniable love that every girl and woman dreamed of.

"Why are you now saying something, Jordyn?" Baylei asked. "You know we are always here for you. I see you every day at work. There's always time to sit and talk about whatever is on your mind."

"I don't want to bother the two of you with dreams I can't control. It seems as if the closer I get to Sanji, the more dreams I have of Lamar. They started off with him just appearing as though he's watching over me. But lately, he's been trying to tell me something. Waking up in cold sweats are starting to scare the hell out of me, and there's nothing I can do about them." A lone tear fell from Jordyn's eye and she quickly wiped it away.

"What do Sanji have to say about these dreams?"

"Toni, I haven't mentioned them to him. How do I go about telling him I'm having dreams about a man that died three years ago? He may not understand, just like I don't. I have no clue as to why the dreams are coming so frequently now."

A thought came to mind, reminding Toni of something her therapist said to her during one of her sessions. "Maybe Lamar is trying to tell you it's okay to move on with Sanji. Knowing you, guilt is eating you up, making you feel as if you're forgetting about Lamar now that Sanji is in your life. If that's the case, you can't do that, Jordyn. Life goes on and you are entitled to be happy. There's life after death, and Lamar wouldn't want you to wallow in pain because he's no longer living."

Jordyn was for sure feeling the guilt of moving on because she made a promise at Lamar's casket to love him forever. She wasn't going to go into detail with her girls because the focus would be on her for the rest of the night. They didn't come out to be on any sad shit, and it was time to change the subject to something happier. Jordyn would figure out how to cope with her dilemma the best she could on her own.

"No, that's not it at all. To tell the truth, I don't know what it is. But enough about me. What's going on with you, Baylei?"

The waitress came over to take their orders and Jordyn sighed with relief. Skimming the menus, the trio finally decided on what they wanted to eat. No one said anything for a few minutes until Baylei broke the silence to fill them in on her life happenings. She ran her hand through her soft curls before tossing them over her shoulder. Baylei looked up at her friends with a nervous smile.

"Y'all know I'm a workaholic, right?" Both Toni and Jordyn nodded their heads yes. "And everybody knows my career means everything to me too, right?"

"Lei, what the hell you trying to get at?" Toni asked irritably. "I hate when you do that shit. Just tell us what's on your mind and we'll go from there."

"Okay. I may be pregnant." Baylei smiled.

"Oh my God! That's great news, Lei!" Jordyn clapped dancing in her seat. "I'm about to be an auntie!" she sang.

"Lei, that's great news! What the hell your career have to do with anything?" Toni asked. "Have you been to the doctor or taken a test?

Baylei shook her head no as she took a sip of water. She opted not to drink any of the wine because she wasn't sure if she was with child or not.

"No, I haven't been to the doctor, nor have I taken a test. The only thing I know is, my period is nineteen days late, and that can only mean one of two things. I'm either extremely stressed, or I'm pretty much pregnant. I truly believe it's the latter."

"Again, why did you mention your career?" Toni pushed.

"This is not the time for me to have a baby. I have a lot of contracts to fulfill, and I want to be there for it all."

"I could understand what you're saying if you were a woman struggling to make ends meet. Lei, you don't need to work another day of your life if you don't want to. Your career is not the reason you're worried about being a mother.'

"It is! There's so much in store for me when it comes to my career! I don't want to put it on hold, Toni. Wes really believed in me when he offered me the position that I'm in."

"We are going to the pharmacy when we're done here. There are plenty of women that work every day while pregnant and haven't missed a beat. Not to mention, you can sketch buildings while sitting on the couch with your iPad. If you like it or not, we will find out if you're having my niece or nephew tahday!"

"What if I want to just have an abortion like it never happened?" Baylei had the gall to say. The question only angered Toni more than her friend's selfishness.

"What if I beat yo' ass and call Mama Anita and tell her what the fuck you thinking about doing? Don't play with me, Baylei, because I will forget you are my sister," Toni sneered. "The way life is set up nowadays, I wish you would let some shit like that fall from your lips again. You will be a great mother, and I'm going to be Super Auntie for the rest of my days."

"I'm just kidding about the abortion part, and I shouldn't have taken it that far. I am worried about working while pregnant because we have more than nine months of work waiting as we speak. Chade is going to have me on bedrest as soon as I share the news with him."

"Lei, your job is secure and you know it. Wes would fly out to handle the company himself to make sure your pregnancy is a breeze. Like Toni said, you can work from home and still be on top of your shit."

"Okay, I hear y'all loud and clear. I guess I'll be finding out if I'm having a baby and figure out what to do about work later," Baylei said rolling her eyes with a smile. "Toni, how's the firm coming along?"

"Girl, Malik is making sure everything is up to par in the building while I've been conducting interviews to fill the place with employees. I can't wait to start doing the kind of work I love because collecting money at the salons is not work in my book. I'm not one of these businesswomen that likes to shop all day and sit in a sunroom with my feet kicked up. I'm a hustla by nature." Toni said raising her glass.

"I'm proud of the accomplishments you have made in such a short period of time."

"Thank you, Jordyn. California is a different ballpark than Chicago and there are a lot of lucrative opportunities for all of us to grow here. We're about to leave our marks in the pavement and we will be known all over in due time."

Their food came at the right moment, and the chatter about Baylei possibly being pregnant ceased. She knew her friends were correct when they said she could work from anywhere. Baylei was going to confirm what she already knew and would have to tell Chade all about it. Their union was one she'd never had. Baylei was beyond happy with Chade. Announcing the new addition to their family would bring an abundance of love into their home.

The waitress walked away, and Baylei picked up her fork to dig into the Jumbo Lump Crab Cakes she'd ordered. The dish was very favorable, but the portion was not enough for the thirty-dollar cost she would have to pay. The money wasn't the issue for Baylei. She just wanted to savor the dish properly. Once finished with the cakes, Baylei started in on her Caesar salad and almost choked on a piece of lettuce.

"Are you okay?" Jordyn asked while patting her friend on the back. Baylei grabbed her glass of water while pointing behind Toni. Taking a sip, Baylei cleared her throat.

"Isn't that Selena?"

Toni and Jordyn both turned their heads to look in the direction Baylei pointed. Sure enough, Selena was smiling hard in the face of a handsome man as if she wasn't a married woman with a baby at home. The way the dude gazed in Selena eyes; one could assume that wasn't their first encounter with one another.

"Um, that's not Samir," Toni whispered lowly.

"It sure as hell isn't," Jordyn said, shaking her head as she watched the guy palm Selena's face.

"Selena and Samir are experiencing a little bit of difficulty," Baylei said after sipping her water for the second time. "I overheard Chade on the phone as he talked to Samir not long ago. He was telling Samir to give Selena time to herself and she would come around. Hell, it doesn't look like she's taking time for self to me. There's no way Selena should be out with another man."

"What the hell happened?" Jordyn asked.

"I don't know, but I think we should go over and invite her out or something. I'm quite sure she needs some positive women in her life right now."

"Lei, I'm not going over there to act friendly with Selena. I really don't give a damn what she's going through. The way she had her nose in the air in St. Thomas, this shit should bring her uppity ass down a few notches."

"Come on, Toni. I understand how you feel, don't get me wrong. But the woman clearly needs someone to talk to before she makes a huge mistake. I'm not asking you to be Selena's best friend. Just be in her corner with me. You would want someone to do it for you."

Baylei knew getting Toni to see things her way was going to be a tough task. Once somebody showed her what they were about, that's the picture she kept in her mind about them. Glancing in Selena's direction, Baylei saw the dude get up and head for the restroom. She took that opportunity to talk with Selena. Since neither of her friends was on board with her, Baylei excused herself and walked across the room to where Selena was sitting.

"Hey, Selena, I thought that was you," Baylei greeted her happily. "How's everything going?"

Selena smiled nervously as she looked around the restaurant. Hoping Chade wasn't around, she locked eyes with Toni and diverted her eyes quickly. She didn't expect to run into anyone affiliated with Samir; especially not when she was with Frank. The last thing she wanted to do was explain what was going on in her marriage.

"I—I—I'm okay. Baylei, right?" Nodding her head yes, Baylei shifted her weight to her other foot to keep her composure. Selena knew damn well who she was, but tried to play dumb. Selena glanced in the direction of the bathroom as she gulped the drink she lifted to her lips.

"Look, I would really appreciate if you wouldn't mention seeing me here tonight. Samir and I are going through something that I can't explain at this time. Believe it or not, I was thinking of a way to contact you. It sucks not having anyone to talk to during a time like this."

"What about your good girlfriend Chasity? I'm quite sure she would hear you out."

Selena rolled her eyes while shaking her head slowly. "That's another story in itself," she said. "I want to apologize for the way I acted on the trip. I judged all of you without even trying to get to know y'all, and that was wrong of me."

"I'm not worried about that, but Toni is another story. Truthfully speaking, she wants to lay hands on you. I won't allow that to happen though, so you don't have to worry about any of that. I don't want to hold you. I just wanted to come over and say hello. Put my number in your phone. We can get together maybe this Saturday to get know one another."

Selena was kind of hesitant as she pulled her phone from her purse. The fact that Baylei revealed how Toni felt had her semi-nervous to accept her invitation. Baylei recited her number as Selena entered it into her phone.

"I sent you a text so you will have my number as well. About Saturday… I'll have to think about that. Tell Toni I'm sorry."

"I promise, Toni won't attack you or anything. You're going to apologize and talk it out with her on your own. We will meet at my home, which you should be familiar with. I'll text the time soon enough. Enjoy the rest of your night."

Baylei turned to leave just as Frank exited the restroom. She turned back to Selena. "To get over someone isn't to get under another. Be safe out here. That one looks kind of fishy."

The departing words Baylei gave Selena resonated in her mind, but she shook it off. Frank was like a breath of fresh air that brought the sunshine back into her life in a week's time. From the outside looking in, many wouldn't understand how that was possible when she had just met the man. With the dark cloud hovering over her head for the past couple months, she needed time to smile and feel wanted. It's not like she was falling in love. In fact, there wasn't any physical contact between them other than a little hug here and there.

Enjoying the time she spent with Frank, Selena figured she would have as much fun as she possibly could no matter what anyone thought or said about her choices. She'd already filed the paperwork for the divorce a few days before. Joyce Little, the attorney, tried talking Selena into counseling after hearing her story, but Selena's mind was set in stone. After hearing that Selena wanted a no-contest divorce, Joyce went through the process and agreed to get the paperwork together as well as mail the documents to Samir via certified mail. The best part was the fact that Selena and Samir wouldn't have to go through drawn-out court proceedings. All he would have to do was sign the papers.

Meesha

Chapter 9

Jordyn made her way home after the three friends went to Walgreens to get a pregnancy test for Baylei. The two of them agreed to head over to Toni and Malik's because he was at the hospital that night. Jordyn passed on finding out because she just wanted to go home and get to bed. Baylei agreed she would call to let her know the results soon as she received them.

The entire ride home, Jordyn thought about everything that happened during dinner and realized she didn't tell her girls about the chic at the firehouse. Maybe it wasn't meant to speak on because it was irrelevant to her. All Jordyn could do was allow Sanji to handle the situation his way. Pulling into her driveway, Jordyn's phone rang and "Daddy" displayed on the car's display. She smiled as she connected the call.

"Hey, Daddy! How are you?" Jordyn asked, smiling harder.

"I'm doing fine, Cupcake. How's life in sunny California?"

"Everything is everything. I miss you and Mommy so much. I've been thinking about coming home for a quick visit soon." The sadness in Jordyn's voice put her father on alert.

"Whenever you're ready, the door is always open for one of my favorite girls. Are you sure you're okay, Cupcake?"

Jordyn bit her bottom lip as her eyes filled with tears. If she couldn't be real with anyone else, her daddy was her definite confidant. There wasn't any way to hide her true feelings from him anyhow. All she had to do was fill in the blanks.

"I miss him so much, Daddy."

Her father took a deep breath because he knew his daughter was going through another episode about Lamar. He took his glasses off and leaned back into his recliner so he could be her listening ear. It had been a few months since Jordyn had called about her past, so he knew she was somewhat healing, but she wasn't quite there yet.

"I've still been having dreams, and now Lamar is trying to verbally speak to me. Maybe he doesn't want me to move on with Sanji. I feel guilty about moving on and don't know what to do."

Jordyn wailed as she struggled to catch her breath. Thinking about Lamar not being alive anymore broke her heart. Waiting for his daughter to gather herself, Jordan sat patiently because he knew how it was when Jordyn had dreams about Lamar. A few moments passed before Jordan decided to speak.

"Dry those tears, Cupcake. I can't tell you how to grieve. You have a new man in your life now. Lamar wouldn't want you to hold on to his spirit. If I recall, he used to say all the time how he wanted to keep a smile on your face. Right now, that smile is not there. I'm sure Lamar isn't happy seeing his Lady Love crying." Jordyn listened to her father's words while wiping the tears from her face.

"From what I've heard, Sanji treats you just as good if not better than Lamar. He has my blessings as a father to be in your life. You will not be able to love that man properly if you don't turn Lamar loose, Cupcake. There aren't any rules which state one cannot love someone who has passed on while loving another. If you talk to Sanji about what's going on, maybe it would you help you through this. Battling these dreams alone will eat you alive, Jordyn."

"He may not understand. Where would I even start?" Jordyn sniffled.

"Start at the beginning. The same way you pour your heart out to me, do the same with Sanji. He will understand; trust me."

"Thank you for always being there for me, Daddy. I love you. Tell mommy I send my love."

"I love you too, Cupcake. You know I'm only a phone call away. Keep me posted on your visit and make sure you bring Sanji along."

"Will do, Daddy."

Jordyn ended the call, feeling a little better. She gathered her things from the passenger side and got out of the car to go inside. Heading straight to her bedroom, Jordyn prepared herself for bed because the crying she had done wore her out. After taking a hot steamy shower, Jordyn didn't bother putting on any clothes as she snuggled under the blanket and allowed sleep to take over.

***

Sanji was dog tired after the night he'd had. It was after eight in the morning by the time he pulled into his driveway. There was a five-alarm fire that came through to the station at three in the morning. Seven firefighters were injured along with a few of the residents that lived in the apartment building. Sanji loved his job, but he hated when there were children were involved. Seeing them crying and scared did something to his heartstrings every time.

Entering the house and locking the door behind him. Sanji was taken by surprise when Jordyn ran across the room and straight into his arms. She was wearing one of his engine 99 shirts that barely covered her ass. His hand automatically palmed it while she hugged him tightly.

"I'm so glad you're okay. I've called you many times since five o'clock. I saw the fire on the news—"

Jordyn spoke rapidly and Sanji halted her words by tilting her head upward, planting a kiss upon her lips. "Jordyn, I'm alright, baby. You will see so many incidents as they unfold via live stream. I want you to know, I signed up to do a job that has been deemed very dangerous, and I enjoy what I do for a living. Worrying is something I never want you to do, but there isn't any way for me to tell you not to do so."

"I was very worried, Sanji. So much that I called Baylei and told her I wouldn't be in the office today." He wrapped his arms around her and kissed her on the forehead,

"I will always come home to you. The only thing you can do is pray for my safe return and know that I will do my job to the best of my ability while making sure I get out unscathed," he whispered in her ear. "Now, go in there, get your gorgeous ass together, and go to work. I'll be here when you return. Don't miss work on account of me. The only thing I'll be doing for the rest of the day is sleeping."

Jordyn wanted to express her feelings at that moment, but decided against it. Hearing Sanji say he would always come home to her did something to her mentally because Lamar said the exact same thing. Then she watched him collapse right before her eyes, so she didn't believe what he said for a minute. Life could happen at the drop of a dime and there would be nothing anyone could do to stop it. Everything in life is already written; we're just acting it out as it's supposed to be. Expecting the unexpected is a hard task that we as people must endure.

Thinking about going to work repeatedly, Jordyn truly didn't want to leave Sanji's side. He must've read her mind because he scooped her into his arms and climbed the stairs heading straight for the bathroom. Sanji placed Jordyn on her feet. There weren't any words spoken as he started the shower. Jordyn watched his every move as he adjusted the temperature of the water.

Sanji stood and turned, admiring his woman with his bottom lip tucked between his teeth. "Allow me to help you out of this," he said, grabbing the hem of the shirt. "As sexy as you look in this Engine 99 gear, the muthafucka is preventing me from seeing the art underneath."

Jordyn's hand immediately covered her stomach and Sanji moved it out the way as he observed her body. Self-consciousness showed each time she was naked in Sanji's presence. With Sanji being physically fit and Jordyn carried a little extra wight in the midsection, she wasn't very confident about her appearance at times. She tried working out on the weekends, but she was very committed, and it didn't seem as if it was really working for her.

"This shit sexy as fuck," Sanji said as he lifted Jordyn onto the counter.

He planted small kisses on her stomach. Falling to his knees, Sanji spread her legs wide and massaged her thick thighs. Running his tongue along her fold, Jordyn's head fell back against the mirror behind her and a low moan escaped her throat.

"This is five-star pussy, bae. I'll go broke for this right here." Sanji smirked as he parted her lower lips with his forefinger and thumb.

As he licked her clit like an ice cream cone, Jordyn was ready to smack him on the top of his head for teasing her. If Sanji didn't know anything, he knew she loved when he gave her head. She leaned forward to go off on him then suddenly, the pressure of his lips clamping down on her bud caused her to fall back against the mirror while clutching Sanji's locs with both hands. The suction alone sent shivers throughout her entire body. The way he was making love to Jordyn's kitty had her bucking against his mouth like a horse.

"Yes, baby, just like that," she moaned, tightening her fists in his hair. "I'm about to cum!"

Sanji stuck his tongue deep in her tunnel and Jordyn's secretions flooded his mouth. He swallowed every drop while continuing to suck on her sensitive pearl. Jordyn tried pushing his mouth away, but he had a death grip on her thighs. Sanji licked her dry and ran his hand down his face as he stood to his feet.

Jordyn's legs were shaking hard against the counter while she struggled to gather herself from the explosive orgasm she'd just experienced. Watching the handsome specimen of man peel his clothes off as if he was an exotic dancer, Jordyn couldn't contain the wetness that oozed out of her yoni as her kitty tingled back to life. She was horny and needed Sanji to rod her out with his dick badly.

Hopping off the counter, Jordyn stepped into the shower without thinking about applying the bonnet that would protect her hair from getting drenched. As soon as Sanji entered behind her, she got down on her knees and kissed the mushroom head of his pipe. His member was standing at attention causing her mouth to water in anticipation of tasting him. Jordyn slid her lips over his dick and relaxed her throat. She had every intention to swallow him whole as if she was an anaconda devouring its prey.

"Mmmmm, shit, J," Sanji growled as he palmed the back of her head.

Jordyn had a long-ass tongue. Her jaws constricted and Sanji had to brace himself against the shower wall as his knees buckled. The wetness of her mouth felt like silk running along his meat. When the tip of her tongue massaged his ball sack, his seeds erupted down her throat and she drank them like milk.

"Awww shit! Fuck, grrrrrr," Sanji growled as his back stiffened. Any other man would've been through after receiving head of that magnitude. Sanji, on the other hand, was ready for another round. He needed to feel the inside of those sugary walls.

"Turn yo' ass around, bend the fuck over, and hug yo' ankles. And you bet' not run from this dick. Payback is a muthafucka, cause you just had me in here sounding like a bitch. I can't let that shit ride."

Jordyn did as she was told, making sure her kitty was exposed from the back. Running her hand from her asshole to between her slit, she looked back at Sanji, and the way he held his lip between his teeth was sexy as hell. Jordyn's kitty was leaking from the tongue lashing he'd put on her and she was ready to feel all of his wood in her love box. Sanji grabbed her hips and guided himself into her yoni. Jordyn gripped her ankles with everything in her so she wouldn't fall forward.

"Mmmmm, shit. Fuck me, baby," she moaned, throwing her ass back on him.

The water cascaded down on her head and Sanji grabbed a handful of her hair, riding her ass aggressively. Every stroke hit a different spot, and Jordyn loved every bit of the loving he was giving her. Their bodies collided vigorously, and Jordyn could feel her orgasm building rapidly. She knew she was about to cum long and hard. When she got that feeling, her pussy was about to have a waterfall effect.

"I'm about to cum, baby."

"Let that shit out then," Sanji said, rising on his toes. "Give me all that pussy, because I'm about to coat your ovaries."

Jordyn's kitty tightened around his pipe and sucked all the seeds out of his sack. Sanji saw flashes of light as he let loose just like he said he would.

"Ahhhhh, ahhhh, yeah," Sanji groaned as he slowed down his strokes. "This is the best pussy in Cali, and the shit belongs to me."

Kissing Jordyn on the side of her neck, Sanji massaged her breasts and the water continued to run. The cool water splashing on her chest hardened her nipples. Sanji lathered a towel with soap and washed Jordyn from head to toe. Finishing their shower, he wrapped her in a towel and carried her into the bedroom, placing her on the bed. Jordyn's eyes closed instantly.

"I changed my mind about you going to work. That was only an appetizer. I'm going in for the full course meal," Sanji said, prying her legs open.

Meesha

Chapter 10

Hayden decided to get up and head to Nitty's Auto Repair to pick up his car. Frank had called and said his vehicle was ready a few days prior, but work got in the way of him making the trip before closing. As he gathered his belongings and requested an Uber on his phone, there was a slight knock on his office door. Hayden glanced up from what he was doing and smiled when his wife, Lacy, appeared in the doorway.

She stood about five feet, six inches, only because of the six-inch heels that adorned her feet. Lacy was a sight to see in the sea green bodycon dress. It complemented her light skin perfectly. Her natural hair had big curls that rested on her shoulders and her baby face was makeup free with only a touch of lip gloss on her luscious lips. Gazing at his wife, Hayden felt his muscle swell in his dress pants.

"Hey, handsome. Where do you think you're going at three o'clock? Your business hours are from eight-thirty 'til six."

"Come on now, wifey. I have to go pick up my side chick. We discussed this the other day and you were cool with it." The smile on Hayden's face didn't waver. He leaned against his desk, waiting for his wife's response.

Lacy placed her hand on her hip with a wicked grin of her own. "I get it. I know what lane to stay in when her ass isn't feeling well. I'm glad she's alright though. Make sure she's clean, oiled just right, and smells fresh, because I can't wait for her to caress my ass when I plant it on her face. I've missed the bitch just as much as you did, baby."

"If anyone else was in this office listening to your crazy ass, they would've actually thought you were talking about a damn woman. You know you are sick in the head, right?" Both Lacy and Hayden laughed as she walked across the room and hugged him.

Lacy and Hayden were married with two children, a set of twin boys that looked like their father was the one who went through nine months of labor and pushed them out. Hassan and Hakeem were fourteen years old. Hayden had to grow up before his time when he found out he was about to be a father. Both he and Lacy were young and had to face the consequences of their action with little time to prepare.

Hayden was eighteen and was set to graduate that year, while Lacy was just a sophomore with two years to go before graduating. Lacy was scared shitless when she arrived at his home to drop the news on him. He, in return, was excited and very happy that they were having a baby. His parents thought they were too young, but accepted the fact they were going to be grandparents. Lacy, on the other hand, didn't have it that easy. Her mother kicked her out of the apartment with the clothes on her back, telling her daughter she was not welcomed back unless she got rid of the baby. Lacy refused and went back to Hayden's parents' house.

Gloria and Hayden Sr. didn't believe in shacking up. They felt bad about the way Lacy's mom turned her back on her child and they didn't have any intentions of doing the same. Instead, they went to pay her a visit and when they returned, a date was scheduled for them to get married the very next day. Lacy's mother met them at the courthouse and gave parental consent for her daughter to marry Hayden and left without a word spoken.

Hayden graduated high school and enrolled into Community College while Lacy continued to attend high school. His parents helped them every step of the way by getting them an apartment and gave them a personal loan of twenty thousand dollars. Hayden worked any job he could land until he found one that he loved, which was doing security. Fourteen years later, Hayden was the proud owner of Vick's Security Corp. Taking his love for security to a whole other level, Hayden provided protection to celebrities all over the world, and his wife was his partner in every aspect of life.

"Before you go, I want to run something by you," Lacy said, stepping away from her husband. She walked behind Hayden's desk and typed away on his computer, finding what she was looking for. "I noticed a few of the invoices don't match the bank deposits. This has been going on for the past six months, babe. This shit just isn't adding up."

Hayden joined his wife and scanned the documents presented to him on the screen. His blood started boiling because he had never had an issue with his money. His best friend Brandon took care of all of his finances, and he knew damn well he wasn't stealing from him. Hayden made a mental note to give his boy a call once he picked up his ride.

"I'll look further into this, Lace. Brandon and I will get to the bottom of whatever is going on. Don't worry about it," Hayden said kissing her lips tenderly. "Do you want me to pick up dinner on the way home?"

"No, I'm going to head home about four. I have to send out the flight information for the guards that are in charge of Mira Adams in New York next week. I'll have dinner ready by the time you get home."

"Sounds like a plan. I love you, Lacy Vick."

"And I love you more, Big Dick Vick," Lacy smirked.

"Yeah, I know what that shit means. You want to fuck tonight. Duly noted, baby mama. I got you."

"I'm nobody's baby mama, Hayden. You know I hate when you say that shit." She rolled her eyes. "Anyway, get outta here so you can be home on time. Oh, I'm sending the boys to your parents' house because I need to be able to scream your name loud as I want."

"Whatever works for you, Sweet Thang. Make sure you call, because you know those two be in the streets more than the young folks," Hayden laughed as he grabbed his briefcase and walked out the office.

Once he walked outside, he pulled his phone out of his pocket when he heard it ding. His ride had pulled up and he hopped inside after checking the license plate, making sure he was getting in the correct car. Hayden dialed Brandon's number as he got comfortable in the back seat. As the driver merged into traffic, Brandon answered on the third ring.

"What's up, Hay?"

"Aye, I need you to go over the books. There's a lot of shit that looks kind of funky with the numbers. I'll be over to your place soon as I handle some business." Brandon was quieter than a church mouse and that sent a red flag straight to Hayden because whenever they talked business, he always had a quick response. At that moment, Brandon was slow to respond, and it didn't sit well with his long-time friend.

"Are you there, B?"

"Yeah, bro. I'm just logging into the system to see what you're talking about. Let me get off here and go through everything thoroughly and get back to you with whatever I find."

"Okay, bet."

Hayden ended the call and shook his head. He knew Brandon wasn't looking into shit because he didn't hear any sounds coming from his end of the call. All he knew was that Brandon better be able to tell him where the fuck his money was when he got to his house, or there was going to be slow singing and flower bringing right then and there.

It took about thirty minutes for the Uber driver to arrive at the auto shop, and Hayden made a vow not to ever use the service again. If he was driving his own vehicle, he would've cut the time in half by taking the back roads. He hated being on anyone's time other than his own, and Lacy's, of course. After thanking the driver, he entered the establishment and walked up to the counter.

"Good afternoon, Hayden." Tasha smiled while batting her eyes at him. "I'll let Frank know you're here."

"Thank you," Hayden replied as he turned and took a seat across the room.

Hayden had been dodging Tasha's advances for years and she still didn't get the hint that nothing would ever transpire between the two of them. She knew he was married, but tried her luck at being his side chick every chance she got. If he was any other dude in the streets, Tasha would've been fucked every which way but up and thrown out with just a wet ass. But he wasn't ,and in the fourteen years that he'd been married, stepping out on his wife was something he had never acted on. The thought crossed his mind every time he saw a woman with a big ass and a pretty face. Then a reminder of what he had at home shut that shit completely down.

"Hayden, Frank would like you to go back to his office," Tasha said, interrupting his thoughts.

With a nod of his head, Hayden stood and made his way to the back of the establishment. As Hayden got closer to Franks office, he could hear his friend laughing while talking to someone. Peeking around the corner, Hayden could see his friend drawing circles on a piece of paper while listening to whoever was on the other end of the line. He knocked lightly on the opened door getting Frank's attention.

"Let me call you back, love. Better yet, I'll see you later for dinner." Saying his goodbyes, Frank ended the call with a smile on his face. "What's up, Vicks? It's about time you came through to get that expensive-ass whip out of my lot, nigga. So many muthafuckas has stopped to inquire if it was for sale. Hell, I should've sold that shit for the low."

"And I would've beat yo' ass," Hayden retorted as Frank came around the desk. They embraced in a brotherly hug and then they both sat down. Clearing his throat, Hayden stared at his homie and watched him gaze at nothing. "Payton must be back home. That's about the only person that can get your mean ass to light up like that."

"Man, I wish she was back. I'm still subjected to phone calls once or twice a week and several pictures to hold me over. Hell, jacking feels like a chore nowadays and a nigga is missing the feeling of pussy like a muthafucka." Frank laughed.

"Well, the way you sounded a few minutes ago, it seems as if it won't be long before you dive into something wet."

Frank laughed as he sat up tall in his chair. The look in his eyes told Hayden that his friend was up to no damn good. He'd been friends with the man sitting before him for damn near two decades and could read him like a book. Frank and Hayden ran the streets of Long Beach when they were younger. That part of his life was still top secret from many in his life, especially his parents. When the odd jobs he worked weren't paying off, Hayden found himself selling drugs on the weekends to make ends meet. With a baby on the way and a wife he wanted to concentrate on school, he had to make shit shake while still being able to prove he was working a legit job.

Before getting married, Frank was a womanizer and dipped off in any female that dropped down to her knees. Payton, his wife, put a stop to that shit; at least, that's what many on the outside looking in thought. Behind closed doors, Frank and his wife always had another woman in their bed. He didn't have to cheat because his woman was down for the cause. She was the one that brought the other women home to him. With Payton being away serving the country, there was no telling what Frank was into.

"Since you're all in my business, I do have a potential in my sights. As a matter of fact, it's the pretty little thang that fucked yo' ride up. We've gone out a few times, and I like her vibe. She hasn't truly opened up to me as of yet, but I'm patient as hell."

"Come on, Nitty," Hayden said, using his street name. "Selena is a good girl and I don't want you to involve her in your shit."

"Man, she's a grown-ass woman. Long as she doesn't fall in love with a nigga, we will be alright. There's nothing wrong with having a little bit of temporary fun. Shit, you know how the fuck me and Payton roll. Selena can be a sister wife if she play her mutha-fuckin' cards right. Payton would love her fine ass."

"She's married, nigga!" Hayden snapped.

"So? I am too. That shit don't mean shit to me. Where the fuck is her husband while she's entertaining my black ass? Since you know so much."

"They're going through some things right now."

"Enough said. She's a free agent. That nigga let a real one come in and occupy his woman's mind. He fucked up. Once I put this dick in her life, there will be no going back." Frank laughed.

Hayden couldn't even be mad at Frank. Selena knew her situation and was doing exactly what she wanted to do. The only problem was the fact she was doing it with a man that had no plans of pursuing anything with her. The things Selena told him about her husband's infidelities weren't shit compared to what she would endure messing around with Nitty. She was better off going back home to her husband, because Frank didn't give two shits about any woman who wasn't Payton.

Hayden left Frank with a lot on his mind. The first thing he contemplated doing was calling Selena to talk some sense into her. He thought about it for a few minutes, but when his phone rang and Brandon's name appeared on the display, all thoughts of Selena and Frank went out the window.

"What you got for me?" Hayden asked once the call connected.

"Everything looks good on my end. I don't see anything out of place. I've printed put everything so you can go over them thoroughly. Highlight anything you catch and I will come right over. Plus, all you have to do is compare shit with your statements. That will tell you all you need to know."

"Have that shit ready for me, because I'm on my way. Brandon, you already know how the fuck I get down. I may have traded my Timbs for Giuseppes, but the same nigga is underneath this shit. If I don't find my muthafuckin' money by tomorrow, you better be long gone."

"Don't threaten me, Hayden. We've been friends far too long for shit to go down like this. I've been your financial advisor since you started this business. Why would I start stealing from you now? You pay me more than any white-collar company I've ever worked and you think I'll fuck that up by taking money from you? Man, come get this paperwork before I say something I'll regret."

Brandon hung up, and that further incriminated his ass. It was his job to work with numbers. Hayden wasn't good at that shit, and Brandon knew it would take him forever to find the error. He had a trick for his ass though. Hayden had to call around to find a trusted advisor to go over his books. When he found out Brandon was, in fact, stealing from him, he would have to send money to his mama to cover his funeral arrangements.

Chapter 11

"Boss Lady, your ten o'clock is here," Chante said, peeking her head in the office door.

Selena had been back at work for the past two weeks, and she missed Sevyn every minute she was gone. Being back in the midst of things kept her mind off her marital issues for the most part. She still hadn't heard anything from Samir pertaining to the divorce, so it was obvious he hadn't received the papers she'd filed. He didn't miss a beat when it came to co-parenting and spending time with their daughter. Selena loved that he kept his word and gave her a break at every turn because she was able to spend more time with Frank.

The time she spent with him brought her so much happiness, and she looked forward to seeing him every time. There was something different about Frank. He wasn't trying to push her into commitment, nor was he forcing her for sexual pleasure. They talked and had fun, enjoying life, just what she needed to get herself together. Jumping into something serious wasn't what Selena wanted at the moment. She needed a friend, and she believed she had that in Frank.

"I'll be out once I find the backdrop I ordered for this shoot," Selena said over her shoulder.

"It's in the cubby by the window on the top shelf."

"Chante, what would I do without you? You are truly a gift from God."

Selena grabbed the items she needed along with a few other props and headed out to the studio. When she entered, she was smitten by the bundle the mother held in her arms. The baby girl was absolutely beautiful. According to the information on the invoice, the little beauty was a month old, her name was Royalty, and she was dark as Nestlé chocolate.

"Oh my God, she is precious!" Selena said gushing over the baby. "The vision you want is perfect for this shoot. Were you able to find the bathrobe, headwrap, and the little flip flops?"

"No! I loved that idea but I couldn't find anything like that. I'm so sorry."

"Nope," Selena said, shaking her head. "There's nothing to be sorry for. I followed my own mind and ordered a set myself in case you couldn't get your hands on it. I'm glad I did."

Selena had the new mother undress her baby and put the items Selena handed to her on the princess. The outfit was purple because the color represented royalty. The little lounge chair Selena made was so cute. Positioning Royalty in the middle of the prop, it looked as if she had taken a bath and passed out afterwards. She looked like a tiny adult who had a long stressful day at the office. That was just one of ten shots Selena had of the baby, but one of her favorites.

The session lasted almost two hours, and Selena was pleased with the results. The mother was in tears looking at the camera roll. She couldn't wait to get her hands on the final print. Making an appointment for the next session, Selena walked her out with a smile.

"That was so cute," Chante said, clapping. "You are back and in full effect! It's like you never left, Selena. You're about to make a name for yourself. I can feel it."

"I hope so. I have so much going on—"

"And you will use every bit of that negative energy to win, Selena. You can't let life take you by the horns and bring you down. I will be here to motivate you every step of the way. This is your winning season; do you hear me? Depression is real and I believe you will get through everything that's happening. Long as you don't give up, you will succeed."

"Thank you so much for that. I really needed to hear every one of those words." Selena had tears in her eyes, but she wiped them away and smiled. "Do I have any more appointments lined up?"

"We have two more in about an hour, and the other at four. I can very well take care of them."

The bell rang, indicating someone at the door. Selena excused herself and went to see who was popping up without an appointment. As she got closer to the entrance, she was surprised to see the person on the other side. It had been a while since she'd seen him, and Selena was curious as to how he'd found her at the studio.

"What a pleasant surprise," she said, opening the door. "How did you know to come here?"

"I have my ways. You're looking good. How have you been?"

"I'm good, Hayden. What brings you here? We've already settled me damaging your car."

Hayden laughed at what Selena said. "My ride is good as new, so that's definitely not what I'm here for. Actually, I wanted to know if you would accompany me to lunch. There are some things I would like to discuss with you." Selena's eyes shifted nervously and Hayden picked up on it immediately. "It's not what you think. My wife is actually in the car as well. This is on a friendship type of level. Nothing more, nothing less."

"I have a few more appointments. Today is not good for me."

"Go ahead, Selena. I have things covered here." Selena cut her eyes at Chante, wanting to strangle her. "Remember what we just discussed. It's a nice day to get reacquainted with friends. You need this outing, Boss Lady."

"I agree with her," Hayden chimed in. "Besides, lunch is on me." He winked.

Selena thought about it for a few seconds. "Okay, let me grab my purse and I'll be ready. I can follow you to the restaurant so you won't have to bring me back to my car."

"Sounds good," Hayden said as he turned and walked back to his car.

Lacy watched her husband's interaction with the woman he found himself worried about since the day she hit his car. Hearing everything Selena was going through, Lacy felt the need to befriend her. She didn't know what it was like to be cheated on, but she could only imagine the pain she was going through.

Hayden invited Lacy to come along because he didn't want Selena to look too much into it when he spoke on her relationship with Frank. Lacy knew firsthand that he wasn't the man she wanted Selena to associate herself with, especially when she'd just left a situation with a man she was married to for years. Frank's wife Payton was cool, but she didn't play when it came to her husband.

"Did she refuse lunch?" Lacy asked as Hayden sat behind the wheel.

"No, she'll be out momentarily. You're going to like Selena. She seems okay, in spite of her dealing with life happenings."

"I just don't want her to fall prey to Frank's hoe ass. There is no telling when Payton will come back. Selena could fall easily into their web and they would turn that woman out!" Selena exited the studio and Lacy whistled lowly. "Yep, I needed to talk to her yesterday, but there's nothing like today. She look's naïve, vulnerable, and she's extremely beautiful. The recipe for disaster when it comes to the Huttons."

Hayden nodded his head in agreement as he put the gear in reverse and pulled out of the parking spot with Selena close behind. The radio volume was low as Kem's "Love Calls" flowed through the speakers, putting them both deep in their thoughts.

"Babe, did you go over the documents Brandon gave you?" Lacy asked after a few minutes of singing. Since her husband owned a car dealership and several residential properties, she wanted him to get to the bottom of the missing funds.

"Yeah, but according to the printouts, things appear to be correct. The numbers on the actual documents is what's not sitting well with me. I'm going to hire someone else that knows what to look for to dig deeper into it. Thanks for reminding me, because it actually slipped my mind. I will make a few calls when we get home."

I'm telling you now..." Lacy turned slightly in her seat. "Brandon is stealing from you. That's your friend, but he's a snake. Brandon hasn't called or come by to ensure everything was alright because he truly thinks he has gotten away with what he has done. You may not be in the streets anymore, but my brothers are. I'm going to leave it at that."

"Lace, we're not going that route. I'm sure I'll be able to get to the bottom of it all. By the way, I can handle my own affairs. You can take the nigga out the ghetto, but you can't take the ghetto out the nigga. I don't need your brothers to handle a damn thang for me. Leave them out of my shit."

Lacy heard what Hayden said. She wasn't trying to hear him though. Her husband was going too easy on his friend, and she felt that that's where he was going wrong with the situation. Depending on the outcome, Brandon was going to be found in the Mojave Desert unrecognizable, if she had anything to do with it.

They pulled up to the restaurant, which caused Lacy to switch her mind from angry to pleasant. The conversation about Brandon was far from over, but she never let the outside world know when she and her husband were in any type of disagreement with one another. One thing Lacy and Hayden stood on was keeping people out of their business and marriage. Many allowed outsiders to become too invested in their affairs and that alone made it easy for the foundation to crumble.

Selena handed the valet driver her keys and made her way to the entrance of the restaurant. She watched as Hayden rounded his car, opening the passenger door. A beautiful woman stepped out, and Selena smiled. Samir used to cater to her attentively all the time. Seeing how Hayden looked at the woman, one could tell he loved her with every fiber of his being.

"Selena, this is my wife, Lacy. Lacy, this is the wonderful woman that bruised my side chick." They all laughed at Hayden's reference as Selena and Lacy shook hands.

"It's nice to meet you. Sorry about the car."

"Don't worry about it. I'm glad you weren't hurt foremost because as you can see, the car was fixed. Material shit can be repaired, but your well-being and life wouldn't have been as easy. I mean, you did bring Hayden to his knees a little bit. He loves that car more than he loves me," Lacy said, looking up at her husband.

"I truly doubt that. The way he admires you says it all. I'm quite sure his car doesn't stand a chance when it comes to you." Selena smiled.

"Well, it's nice to meet you too. I don't know about you, but this girl is hungry."

"Lead the way, Mrs. Vick. It's your world, I just live in it."
Hayden winked, ushering the women toward the door.

The trio was seated promptly and they were able to look over
the menu then ordered thereafter. Hayden and Lacy sat on one side
of the table as Selena got comfortable on the other. She was extremely nervous when around someone she really didn't know.
Selena was still curious as to why Hayden showed up at her studio
for this lunch date. He must've read her mind because shortly after,
he got to the point she was thinking about.

"Selena, I've been worrying about you since the day we met,"
Hayden said, draping his arm around Lacy's shoulder. Selena's eyebrow rose in confusion because to her, it sounded some funny stuff
was about to fall from his lips that she wasn't going to like one bit.

"Stop looking at me that way." He laughed. "I wanted to make
sure you were cool. That's all. How's things going with you and
your husband?"

Selena sat back with a sigh. She should've known Hayden
would bring up Samir, seeing that was all he knew about her other
than she wrecked his vehicle. "We're co-parenting. I went ahead
and filed for divorce, but my soon-to-be ex-husband hasn't uttered
a word about the matter as of yet. I'm a single woman enjoying life,
taking care of my daughter, and back running my business full-time.
Life goes on after divorce." Selena said and smiled.

Hayden noticed Selena appeared genuinely happy and held her
head high as she gave a brief rundown. The weight of the situation
had lifted tremendously and the light was shining bright in her eyes.
He could tell when someone was trying to cover up happiness, but
he didn't see that with Selena. Hayden hated that Frank probably
had something to do with the change she had made.

"I was married four years and I thought Samir would be my
forever. Obviously, I thought wrong. My forever fucked someone
that was temporary, and it cost him everything. Siting back moping
around was something I wasn't too fond of doing. So, I met someone and have been having the time of my life."

Lacy glanced at Hayden, wondering if he was going to speak
on Frank at that point. When he didn't, she folded her hands on top

of the table, leaned forward and looked Selena in the eyes. There was no way she was going to allow this woman to ruin herself with a man that wasn't about anything.

"I'm about to speak woman to woman with you, Selena. I know you and your husband are going through a rough patch and you made the decision to leave the marriage. There's nothing wrong with that because you didn't see yourself being with a man that would step out on you. Understandable. But I want you to hear me out, and there isn't any judgement coming from me. You can't move on with someone new until you get over the last one. I see—"

"I'm not moving on with Frank." Selena slipped up by revealing the name of the person she was entertaining.

"Frank?" Hayden and Lacy said in unison as if they didn't know who had her smiling from ear to ear.

"There's a lot of Franks in the world, but please tell me you're not talking about Frank Nitty, the owner of the auto shop?" Hayden inquired.

Selena took in their reaction and didn't get a good vibe from the couple at all. She might as well fess up and confirmed that Frank was indeed the person she was dating because being ashamed was something Selena was not. Hayden and Lacy seemed to know Frank beyond working on their vehicle and didn't appear to be too pleased about the news she'd shared.

"Yes, that Frank," Selena finally replied. "I went to the shop to pay for the damages to your car, Hayden. Frank asked me out for lunch, and we hit off. It's nothing serious. We're still getting to know one another."

"I don't have the right to tell you who to spend time with, but be careful with Frank. Keep things on a friendly level; nothing more," Hayden said, taking a sip from his glass of water.

"See, my husband is beating around the bush. I'm going to give it to you straight up. Frank is—"

"Not your business, Lace." Hayden cut his wife of mid-sentence while rubbing her back. "I said the important statement. Leave it at that. It's up to Selena to take heed."

"Hayden, if there's anything I need to know about Frank, please enlighten me. Fuck that, how do you know him?" Selena asked quizzingly.

"Frank and I ran with the same crowd back in the day. I've known him for years, and I will admit he has changed for the better in many ways. I wouldn't sit here and say he's a bad guy, because he's not. But Frank isn't a good companion to women," Hayden explained. "All I'm saying is this, don't take whatever y'all doing past friendship. Meaning, leave the benefits part out of the equation one hundred percent."

"In other words, leave that nigga alone!" Lacy sneered. "You're not ready for the bullshit Frank has to offer. Hayden won't tell you, but I'm a woman before anything. Frank is married. What my husband meant to say was, Frank isn't a good companion to *any* woman that's not his wife. If you're trying to better yourself after your husband's infidelity, you are better off being alone or work that shit out at home. Frank isn't the solution to your problem."

The glare Hayden shot at his wife scared Selena, but Lacy didn't seem to be worried at all. She opened her mouth to speak and Hayden cocked his head to the side, causing Lacy to roll her eyes. Hayden felt his wife had said too much for his liking. Had he allowed her to go on, Lacy would've revealed plenty more where Frank and his wife was concerned. It wasn't her place to do that though.

"Frank will tell you whatever you want to know about him. He's a pretty standup guy when it comes to honesty."

"Hayden, he's only straight up if the shit is asked. Any standup nigga would've told this woman about his wife the moment he asked her out," Lacy spewed venom with each word she spoke. "And stop looking at me like that! I'm only telling her what she needs to know. Plus, she needs a bitch like myself by her side so she won't make the worst mistake of her life by falling for Frank Hutton with his sex crazed ass!"

"Lacy, that's enough," Hayden growled, low enough for only the people at their table to hear.

The waitress came over in the nick of time with their food. This gave everyone the opportunity to take in the conversation that had taken place. The steak Selena wanted so badly didn't make her stomach smile like she hoped. The things she'd heard had her second guessing what she thought was going on between her and Frank. Selena ate slowly as she listened to Hayden and Lacy talk about their businesses. Her phone sounded from her purse, taking her attention away from their conversation. Selena wiped her hands as she retrieved the device from her purse. Seeing Samir's name on the display, she declined the call and sent him a text instead.

Selena: I'm having lunch with some friends at the moment. What's up?

Samir: Call me when you get home. I just received some papers in the mail. Is this what you really want to do, Selena?

Selena: You got the papers, right? Of course, this is what I want to do. My mind was made up when you decided to step out on this marriage. There's no turning back Samir. Sign the papers and send them back. Then you can go out and fuck whomever you want without feeling guilty.

Samir didn't respond to her last message, and Selena held the phone waiting for his reply. When there was no other interaction on her phone, she chucked it back in her purse and continued to eat. She sat talking with Hayden and Lacy while eating and actually enjoyed the conversation and company they were having. Frank wasn't brought up again and Selena was glad because it was better without all extra intensity of the subject.

Meesha

Chapter 12

Samir sat reading over the divorce papers that were delivered by certified mail. On one hand he was mad because Selena didn't even want to even try to make their marriage work. On the other, he felt he was wrong for being upset that she presented the papers and wanted to move on with her life. The one thing Samir didn't want to do was hold on to a woman that didn't want to be kept.

He got up, went to his office, and fetched a pen before going back to the living room. He read over the documents and agreed with the terms Selena wanted. Everything was reasonable, and she wasn't asking for much. Samir signed the papers without hesitation before placing them back in the envelope to be mailed out.

When Samir decided to text Selena about the divorce papers, he was in his feelings and wanted to try and talk her into going to counseling. Her response took him out and put clarification on what she had verbally said months back. Nothing had changed. The only thing Samir could do was be there for Sevyn and be the best father he could possibly be without going back and forth with Selena in a negative manner.

Samir had witnessed so many men battling with the mother of their kids because they didn't want to be in a relationship with them anymore. He didn't want to be one of those men because the child ended up being the one hurt in the end, and Samir didn't want that for his daughter. Even though he didn't like the way things played out, he was going to prepare himself to be a part-time dad, since he wouldn't be able to live under the same roof full-time with his daughter.

With an outstretched hand, he grabbed his phone from the coffee table and leaned back onto the couch. Contemplating if he wanted to text Selena for the last time or not, he closed his eyes with a deep sigh. He lifted his head and went to the text thread between himself and his soon-to-be ex-wife.

Samir: Selena, I want you to know that I signed the papers and will honor your wishes. Thank you for being a loving wife for the past four years and a great partner throughout the entire courtship.

I will be forever grateful to call you the mother of our daughter. Stepping out on our marriage was the worst thing I've ever done and I will have to deal with that decision every day of my life. It's going to be hard being apart from you because I felt we were in this thing together and I fucked it up.

You have a bright future ahead of you. Don't allow my indiscretions stop you from going further up the ladder in the photography world. Your name will shine bright if you keep pushing for the stars. I'm writing this to release my pain because I know you always had my back and I failed you. Whoever you end up with, make sure he values you as the Queen you are. Don't let him treat you less than you deserve. Demand the upmost respect. Love is a beautiful thing, Selena. Love is also painful when you love someone enough to walk away.

I remember when you told me about praying for a loving man like myself. Now, I'm praying for you and Sevyn to be happy. To find a man who finds a new partner in you. As much as I would love to be friends with you after this, I know new beginnings comes with new ends. This is our end, Selena. Sevyn will always connect us. This is not a goodbye, but a Thank you for everything.

Samir's thumb hovered over the arrow to send the message and tears rolled down his face. He was biting his bottom lip hard enough to draw blood. Pressing that button would be validation that he would no longer be a married man, and the shit hurt like hell. Without thought, Samir pressed the button and threw his phone on the table. He walked upstairs and headed straight to the bathroom. Samir looked at himself in the mirror and grimaced. His hair was unkept as well as the beard he had grown out in the past couple weeks. He brushed his teeth before reaching for the clippers that were lying on the countertop. It was a brand-new day and he wasn't going to sit back wallowing in despair another day. Selena made her choice and he closed out that chapter in his life. Not that he wanted to do so, but it's what she wanted.

***

Walking into the bar, Samir sat on a stool and waved down the bartender for a drink. Staying in the house after grooming himself and taking a nice hot shower was out of the question. He had been sitting around sad since Selena left because he didn't want to look as if he was celebrating her being gone. Now, she had started the process of being single and it was time for Samir to enjoy life. He wasn't out to find a woman. That was the furthest thing from his mind. Samir just wanted to enjoy a night out amongst other people then go home and sleep without any worries.

"What can I get you, handsome?" the petite woman asked as she waltzed in front of him with a crop top on that barely covered her perky breasts. Her smile was far and wide, showcasing a mouthful of beautiful teeth.

"Get me a Henny on the rocks with a bottle of Heineken, please."

Samir looked around the bar and zoomed in on the person that was singing on stage. When he walked in, there was a R&B joint on, but he didn't notice there was karaoke going on. The woman sounded like she was howling to the moon, and it was hard on everybody's ears. Some of the folks were laughing while others tried booing her off the mic. It didn't work because she finished the song and took a bow as if she was a celebrity.

"Here you go." The bartender smiled. "That will be twelve dollars."

Samir turned and threw back his drink. "Let me get two more of those and run a tab, beautiful." Doing as she was told, the bartender left to pour Samir's drinks. Hating to be center of attention, Samir drank from the bottle of beer as he contemplating putting his name on the list to sing. When he got his other shots, he downed one and got up and maneuvered his way through the crowd of people. He decided to add his name and enjoy the night.

About thirty minutes later, Samir was tipsy as hell and swayed through to the beat of the music. One dude sang "Pretty Wings" by Maxwell and tore the house down. Women were fanning themselves because that man could sing his ass off. The announcer got on the mic and called Samir's name to come up next. He was nervous as hell because there was no way he could go on after the previous act.

"Samir, where you at playa? I know you ain't chickening out because Mike just blew these women away." Everyone was looking around laughing as they tried to figure out who Samir was. One thing he didn't turn away from was a challenge.

Making his way to the stage, Samir finished off his beer and placed the bottle on a nearby table. He climbed the steps and adjusted the mic to his liking. When the music for "Tennessee Whiskey" started playing, everyone looked around with "what the fuck" expressions on their faces. Every person before him had sang something from an African American artist. Samir was stepping outside the box to sing what his heart desired. As he bellowed out the first note of the song, the crowd went wild.

Used to spend my nights out in a ballroom
Liquor was the only love I've known
But you rescued me from reaching for the bottom
And brought me back from being too far gone

You're as smooth as Tennessee whiskey
You're as sweet as strawberry wine
You're as warm as a glass of brandy
And honey, on your love all the time

I've looked for love in all the same old places
Found the bottom of the bottle always dry
But when you poured out your heart I didn't waste it
'Cause there's nothing like your love to get me high

You're as smooth as Tennessee whiskey
You're as sweet as strawberry wine
You're as warm as a glass of brandy
And honey, on your love all the time

Samir poured his heart out with every word spoken because the song got him through many days of drinking and sulking. He wanted to sing the words one last time to get that part of his life out of his mind so he would move on. Samir's rendition of Chris Stapleton's song took the atmosphere of the club to a whole other level. The crowd was singing with him even though they were skeptical about his song choice at first.

When he sang the last note, the crowd erupting in applause. The announcer played the instrumental back and "encore, encore" was shouted throughout the room. Samir shook his head no and thanked the crowd as he handed off the mic and made his way back to the bar. He was stopped several times with back pats and hugs by the time he returned to the stool he had vacated earlier. The bartender came right over and placed two more shots of Hennessey in front of him without asking, but he thanked her all the same because that was what he was about to do anyway.

"You sounded great up there. Good job," she winked.

"Thank you."

The alcohol was running through Samir's bloodstream, but he didn't want to stop because it kept his mind clear of the life events he was going through. Samir knew drinking wasn't the answer to his problems. It did keep him from being down and that was the last thing he wanted. Samir wanted to have fun. Nothing more, nothing less.

Shifting in his seat, Samir saw the silhouette of a woman with wide hips and a small waist pulling the stool next him out so she could sit. In his mind he had gotten up to help, but in reality, he did no such thing. He was drunk as hell by that time and was wondering how the hell he would get home. Samir's head was spinning and he could barely hold it up.

"Hey, are you okay?"

"Damn, an angel is talking to me," Samir laughed as he struggled to clear his blurred vision. Fumbling around for his bottle of beer, he accidently knocked it over, spilling the contents onto the counter.

"Whoa, you've had enough. Hey, Shantrice, bring me a glass of water please."

Samir laid his head on his arms because it was too heavy. He'd never gotten so drunk while out by himself, and he was embarrassed. The unknown woman shook his arm vigorously, and it made him kind of nauseous in the process.

"Come on, drink this," she said, lifting his head. "My name is Summer and I'm going to make sure you get home safe and sound. Is there anyone I can call to come get you?"

Summer looked down at his hand and realized he wore a wedding band on his left ring finger. She felt his pockets until she felt what she hoped was his phone. Attempting to get it out of his jeans, Samir smirked as he turned to face her.

"Be careful, beautiful. That pistol is loaded and ready to shoot."

Summer laughed and pulled out the phone. Swiping up on the screen she noticed it was locked and needed Face ID to unlock it. Samir had put his head back down on the counter, making it hard for Summer to complete the task of opening his phone. She tapped him on the shoulder and when he lifted his head, Summer used the opportunity to unlock the phone. Scrolling through his contacts, she happened upon the name "Wifey" and prayed the outcome was a good one. The phone rang a few times, but the voicemail picked up. Summer decided not to try his wife again because she didn't need the drama in her life. Instead, she chose the contact that read Chade and knew she couldn't lose with that one.

"Samir, what's going on, bro? It's after midnight."

"Um, this isn't Samir. My name is Summer and who I now know is Samir is here at Kool Karaoke. He is pretty wasted and won't be able to drive home. Would you be able to come pick him up before something horrible happens to him?" Summer bit her nail as she waited for a response.

"Yeah. Thank you for calling. I'm on my way. Give me about thirty minutes and I'll be there. Don't let him leave under any circumstances."

"I won't. It would defeat the purpose of me tracking someone down to come get him. He's in good hands until you arrive."

Summer ended the call and held on to Samir's phone. He was snoring lightly and would probably need to be carried out of the bar. As she watched Samir like a hawk, his cell phone vibrated with a text. *Wifey: Samir, I don't feel like talking about the divorce. If it's not about Sevyn, please don't call me at this time of the night. I read your last message and I'm glad you're not fighting me on this. Goodnight.*

Summer had an inkling as to why Samir was drunk the way he was. He was going through a divorce and his soon to be ex-wife wanted nothing more to do with him. The situation was sad as hell, but she was not the type to judge. Whatever happened had to be bad because she didn't even answer the phone, but she texted instead. Regardless of what was going on between them, the man was the father of her child and any-thing could be wrong with him. Which it was. Summer didn't know the extent of their issue so she shook her thoughts out of her head.

She knew after Chade arrived, there would be no way she would see the handsome guy again. She wanted to be able to check on him, and he wasn't in any condition to give her his information. What Summer had in mind would come off as stalkerish to most people, but there was no way she was going to lose contact with the handsome man sleeping in front of her. Calling her phone from his, she locked the number in for later use.

Exactly thirty minutes later, Samir's phone rang in Summer's hand. Chade was calling and she answered abruptly. "Hello," she said with her finger inside of her ear.

"I'm on my way inside. Where exactly are you and Samir?"

"At the bar on the main level," Summer replied.

"Okay, bet."

Summer watched the door and two handsome men walked inside, looking around aimlessly. When they started walking in the direction of the bar, she knew those were Samir's people. Summer nudged him and he shifted slightly, but didn't wake up.

"Are you Summer?" Summer nodded her head up and down as she salivated over the fine men that stood before here. "What's wrong? You can't talk now?" Chade asked.

"S-sorry. Yes, I'm sorry."

"Who are you and how did you know to call me?"

"I didn't know, but I called who I'm going to assume is his wife and she didn't answer. She texted him back though," Summer said with a frown. "Please get him out of here. He's had too much Hennessey."

Chade was mad hearing that Selena didn't come through for Samir. He didn't have time to dwell on the whatnots. He just needed to get him out of this bar looking like a drunken solicitor. Walking behind his friend, Chade gripped Samir's shoulders and pulled him upright.

"Samir, get up, my dude."

Samir's eyes rolled around for a minute as he focused on the person standing beside him. "Chade, what's going on, bro? I think I had too much to drink," he slurred.

"You think? The shit is coming out your pores as if you poured that shit on yourself for aftershave. We don't do this shit solo, man. What were you thinking?"

His head fell to his chest and Chade couldn't do anything other than shake his head. Summer got up from the stool so the other guy could stand on the other side of Samir. The two of them grabbed Samir under his arms and hoisted him up from the stool. The bartender came over before they could head for the door.

"Sorry, but he has a tab running. Who's going to pay it?"

"Damn, bro," Chade said trying to reach his wallet. "How much is it?"

Looking down at the receipt she said, "a hundred fifty."

"You muthafuckas don't have a cut-off around here? How the hell do y'all let somebody get fucked up and still pushing drinks at 'em? Change yo' policy, because this is how folks end up not making it home!"

Chade threw his card on the counter and waited for the bartender to return with it. Even though he was upset, he still gave her ass a hefty tip because she was only doing what she was paid to do. He then turned to Summer and she held out a phone to him.

"Thank you for looking out for my people," Chade said, going back into his wallet to give her some money.

"You don't have to do that. I'm glad there was someone who cared enough to come get him. If push came to shove, I would've taken him home with me until he sobered up. I despise drunken drivers, and I wouldn't have gotten any sleep worrying if he made it home safely."

"That's what's up. I'm glad he was here with you."

"No, he wasn't with me. I don't even know him." Summer laughed. "Just call me the good Samaritan that cares about the life of others. Y'all go ahead and get him to bed. Thanks again for caring."

Summer turned and disappeared into the crowd. Chade stared in the direction she had gone and smiled. "That was a good-ass woman," he said to himself as he and Vincent helped Samir out of the bar.

Meesha

Chapter 13

Baylei was awakened out of her sleep the night before when Chade told her he had to go out and get Samir. It took him over an hour to come back to the house and it was a mess. She didn't sign up to be Nurse Betty, but she wasn't the type of woman to leave a person hanging. Baylei stood while Samir threw up all the liquor he'd consumed at the bar without any complaints. The only issue was, every time he threw up, she ran to the other bathroom to do the same.

"Bae, I'll take care of Samir. You go in there and lay down. Thank you for helping me out." Chade embraced Baylei and kissed her on the forehead. "Brush your teeth and I'll give you a real kiss. I love you, but not enough to share your vomit."

Baylei laughed as she tried kissing Chade on the lips. "No, for real, I understand. That's some nasty shit. Put Samir in the guest room and make sure he has a garbage can next to the bed. I'm not cleaning up anything behind him. Have you called Selena?" she asked.

"Selena isn't fucking with Samir right now. The chick that called me called her first and she didn't answer. Instead, she sent him a text. When Samir sobers up, I'm going to see what's going on with that. I'll try to wrap this up quick as possible so I can come give you some of this natural melatonin to put you to sleep," Chade smirked.

Baylei blushed and pushed him out of the room before closing the door. She walked into the closet and pulled the pregnancy test out of her purse. When she and Toni went to Walgreens, she opted to take the test when she got home. That didn't happen because she wasn't ready to confirm what she already knew. Her period was late and the nauseousness was overwhelming. There was no way she wasn't pregnant. All the signs were there.

Entering the bathroom, Baylei sat on the toilet and opened the test. When she started urinating, she put the stick in the stream and put the cap back on and set the test on a piece of tissue. Wiping herself, she washed her hands and waited. Baylei brushed her teeth while waiting to read the results. Taking a deep breath as she picked up the stick, clear as day the two pink lines stood out like a neon sign. She was happy but at the same time, she was still worried about how she would handle being pregnant and work. She stood staring at herself in the mirror when the door opened.

Chade stood in the doorway and Baylei tried pushing the test out of his view. She wasn't fast enough. He walked inside and grabbed her around the waist while reaching for the stick with his right hand.

"What do we have here?" he asked curiously. Looking down at the test, a big smile appeared on Chade's face. "Is this real, Lei? You pregnant?" Baylei nodded her head yes and Chade picked her, swung her around, and kissed her passionately.

"You just made me the happiest man in the world right now! I'm about to be a muthafuckin' daddy! I love you so much, Baylei." Chade had tears running down his face as he stared at the test. "Not in a million years have I ever thought I'd be in this position. Thank you so much."

Baylei saw the excitement in Chade's eyes and that alone made her happy to be pregnant. Keeping a smile on her man's face was her ultimate goal. She would just have to talk to him about her work concerns and go from there. There was no way she was going to rain on his parade by complaining about working while pregnant.

"You don't have to thank me. It was bound to happen, Chade. You were humping on me every chance you got like a jack rabbit. So, I take it you are happy I'm pregnant."

"Hell yeah, I'm beyond happy! I'm about to be able to groom my namesake. Boy or girl, it doesn't matter to me. One thing I do know, my mama is about to be ecstatic when she hears this news. She has been hounding me to give her grandbabies for the longest time."

"I hope Miss Capri is gonna be happy with one grandchild, because this isn't happening again," Baylei said walking out of the bathroom. She climbed in the king-sized bed and got under the covers.

"Lei, you haven't even started the pregnancy experience yet. You may love the process and want more babies."

"That's a no for me. Being nauseous is enough for me. I'm good."

Baylei snuggled under the covers and Chade walked around to the other side of the bed. Taking off his joggers, he got in and cuddled with Baylei, holding her from the back. The pajamas she had on were too much for his liking and he wanted her to come out of all the extra material.

"Why you got on these clothes?"

"I'm in bed, Chade." Baylei chuckled as she scooted her butt back on him. "I'm sleepy and I think I'm going to be too tired to go into the office. With you and Samir waking me, it's going to be hard for me to fall asleep."

"Nah, it's not. I told you I had some melatonin that would take you right to Lalaland. Are you up for it?" he asked, nibbling on her neck.

She didn't answer, so Chade took it upon himself to dive under the covers and removed her pajama bottoms. Spreading her legs, he parted her lower lips and dove in head first. Baylei palmed the back of his head as he enjoyed his midnight snack.

***

Chade woke up and decided to make lunch for Baylei, since both of them had slept in. As he walked down the stairs, Chade noticed Samir sitting at the island with his head in his hands. When he heard his friend approaching, Samir turned slightly, and Chade immediately noticed the stress lines on his face along with the fact he was extremely hungover. Taking a seat next to Samir, Chade would wait for him to start talking before he made any type of food.

"How did I get to yo' crib, fam? I looked outside and my car is out there, but I don't remember driving here."

"That's because you didn't. I had to come pick you up from the bar last night. Samir, since when have you gone out alone and got that fucked up? We don't do shit like that, man."

"Yeah, I know," he said, rubbing his hands over the top of his fade. "Yesterday I received a certified envelope and it was divorce papers from Selena. I prepared myself for the moment, but I truly didn't think she would go through with it. The shit fucked me up bad and I got fresh and went out to have a good time. Hell, it's been months since I smiled sincerely. It seemed like when I signed those papers, a weight was lifted off my chest. Then again, the shit hurt like hell. I had no intentions of getting messed up last night. I even joined in on the fun and sang karaoke." He laughed thinking back on his performance. "How did you know to come get me?" Samir asked.

"This fine-ass woman hit my line and told me where you were. When I arrived, I thought you were there with her at first. She cleared that up and come to find out, she was your guardian angel at the right place, at the right time, looking out for you. When I say you were fucked up, you were fucked up. Head on the bar counter and all. You almost got yo' ass put out on the side of the road when you almost threw up in my ride. Vincent rode with me and drove your car over here."

Samir didn't remember any of that and was embarrassed for being out in public wasted. He didn't have any recollection of any woman he interacted with at the bar. Another wave of sadness washed over him as he took a deep breath.

"I'm sorry you had to see me like that, Chade. Shit hasn't been easy for me and I should've called one of y'all to kick it with me. I've been drinking like that at home, but never in the streets. Maybe now that everything is about to be finalized, I can get back to being myself. The only thing I'm worried about now is being a father to Sevyn and finding another fucking job."

"That's all you can do, Samir. Selena wants to be set free, and I'm glad you're not fighting her on this. Summer called her and she let the call go to voicemail before sending you a message. I don't know what the message said, but that's how I came into play. It's all about Sevyn at this point. I thought you were waiting for your boss to get back with you about the investigation."

"I was. I actually got a call this morning from him. Mr. Whittaker said he hated the decision he had to make, but he didn't have a choice except to let me go. He also said he knows I didn't have anything to do with the criminal activity that Lavita was involved in, but I was involved with her on a personal level, and that was against company policy. He asked me to come to the branch to pick up documents about my severance pay he put together for me. That will probably be little or nothing, but I can't blame anyone but myself. Not only did I lose my wife behind this shit, I lost my fucking job. The pussy wasn't worth all this."

Chade felt bad for his boy and couldn't find the words to say to him. He stood and went into the kitchen to cook. He decided to make spinach and egg paninis for lunch. As he walked around gathering ingredients for the meal, Samir started talking again.

"Selena has never left me out there like she did last night. The message put the nail in the coffin for me. She didn't even respond to the long as message I sent before I went out. I poured my heart into that shit." Samir looked off into space without blinking. Then he shook his head and laughed lowly. "I guess I have to learn to be my myself for a while, huh? Aye, Summer is the name of the chick that called you? What she look like, and did you get a number so I can thank her?"

Chade smirked at Samir as he cut up the spinach. "Man, you don't need to get involved with someone else right now. Summer was bad though. Baby girl is a beautiful sight to any man that laid eyes on her. She's stacked in all the right places and she looks as if she is on her shit, but looks can be deceiving. Look how Chasity had Ahmad fooled. I didn't get a contact number on her. I was too busy trying to get yo' drunk ass out of there." At that moment Baylei entered the kitchen and Chade thought she only caught the ass end of the conversation.

"Samir, if you want to go out and explore something new, do that shit. Just don't rush anything because your feelings are still with Selena. It's not my business, but a brother to Chade is a brother to me. We got off on the wrong foot in the beginning and we got over that. One thing I don't like to see is someone staying loyal to somebody that don't care how the other is feeling. That's exactly what I see in Selena. She has already started dating again. Why can't you?"

Samir was shocked to hear that Selena was back in the dating field, but it explained her actions more clearly. He understood she wanted to be free to do her after what he'd done and he couldn't even be mad. Going out and mingling should have been his ultimate goal, but that's not what he wanted to do. It was a new ball game now that he knew his soon-to-be ex-wife was living her best life while he was sulking over her ass. After he ate, he would head to the branch to see what Whittaker had for him. Then he was going to get Sevyn before heading home to start his job search.

"Baylei, don't encourage him to go out there and earn his hoe card back." Chade laughed. "Why you playing hooky from work?"

"The same reason you're still here. Freaky-ass negro. Had you not had me up until three this morning, maybe I would've been able to get up."

Samir laughed at their bickering. "Y'all was in there tearing that bed up. I guess both of you forgot you had an uninvited guest in the other room."

Baylei's face turned beet red at Samir's revelation of their sex session. She cut her eyes at Chade, then slapped him in the back of the head when he laughed. He hugged her around the waist and kissed her lips while rubbing her stomach.

"I see that baby is going to have you trying to get away with being abusive," Chade joked.

"Baby?" Samir's eyes bucked. "Are congratulations in order?"

"Yeah, I knocked her ass up without trying. Baylei is officially my baby mama."

"Correction. I will never be a baby mama, Chade. The mother of your child, yes. But never a baby mama. Don't repeat that shit to another soul. You may get your feelings hurt in public. As a matter of fact, let me go make a doctor's appointment. That test may be faulty."

"Stop dreaming, woman. You're carrying my seed, and that test is accurate than a muthafucka. You 'bout to have my baby," Chade sang as Baylei walked out the kitchen.

The past couple months had been good for Chade. His life has taken a turn in the right direction since meeting Baylei. The feeling

124

of being a family man had him walking around with his chest poked out. Now, he had to figure out a way to get Samir back to the man he knew him as because the one sitting before Chade was spiraling out of control. One thing he wouldn't do was allow his boy to hit rock bottom over a few bad decisions he had made.

Meesha

Chapter 14

Samir left Chade's and decided to call Mr. Whittaker and make sure he was at the branch. His clothes were disheveled, but he didn't really care because he was out of a job anyway. Dressing to impress just to get his walking papers wasn't part of his plan. Samir was already upset for going out and getting drunk the night before. Not knowing exactly what he'd been through during that time was eating him up.

Entering the place he'd spent the past nine years giving his all felt foreign to Samir. He was greeted by former colleagues and some of the clients as well. Samir fought hard not to shed a tear. He had trained and groomed his crew to dominate the banking field. Then he was given the boot. That's what bad decisions did to some folks.

"Samir, how are you doing, son?"

Samir looked at his former boss like he had shit on his face as he walked toward him. He had to check his attitude because everything that had taken place was caused because of his actions alone. Samir couldn't blame anyone except himself; definitely not Mr. Whittaker. If it wasn't for him, Samir wouldn't have been highly sought out by clients. He was given the foundation and he captivated off of Mr. Whittaker's guidance.

"I'm maintaining," Samir sighed. "I figured I'd come in to close this chapter of my life."

Seeing a hint of sadness in his protégé's eyes, Mr. Whittaker patted Samir shoulder and nodded his head. "Walk with me," he said, leading the way to the office he only used occasionally. Samir took a seat while Mr. Whittaker retrieved an envelope from the file cabinet.

"Samir, you are a great man and an even better leader. The decision I had to make was hard because I'm losing one of my top managers and financial advisors. What you did wasn't horrible, but it went against company policy. Not to mention, it wasn't very professional. I don't want any of the other employees to think it's okay to fraternize on the job."

"No one knew what was going on with me and Lavita, Sir."

Mr. Whittaker's eyebrow rose in surprise. "Just because it was quietly kept from you. Majority of the staff knew about your involvement with Miss Levitt. She didn't keep the encounters between the two of you private."

Samir sat pondering what was said and he wanted to choke the hell out of Lavita's messy ass. She was lucky to be in jail. Mr. Whittaker cleared his throat and Samir shook the thoughts out of his head.

"I put a package together for you. The contents are one I've never done before, but you deserve every bit of it, Samir."

Mr. Whittaker slid the envelope in front of Samir, motioning him to open it. Inside, Samir was granted one year's pay, plus the vacation and sick days he had accumulated. He was also able to keep the insurance at the same price as employees during that time as well. There was also a letter of recommendation signed and dated by Mr. Whittaker himself. The severance package was impeccable and Samir was very grateful of what he had received. Any other job would've left him in the dirt to fend for himself. with what he was given, Samir had plenty of cushion to find another job without worry.

"Thank you so much. I really appreciate you doing this for me."

"No thanks needed. All I ask is for you to make wiser decisions. Hopefully, you have learned a valuable lesson, Samir. Lavita was the wrong person for you to deal with. Any woman other than your wife for that matter. Make things right at home because a happy wife, a happy life. Live by that."

Samir wasn't trying to get into his personal business. He was aiming to forget about the turmoil he'd created for the time being. The two men talked for a few more minutes before Samir left the branch feeling a lot better than when he entered.

It was a nice day and he wanted to enjoy it with his baby girl Sevyn. When Samir sat in his car, he connected his phone to the Bluetooth and called Selena. The phone rang a few times before going to voicemail. As he attempted to call again his phone rang with an unknown number. Curiosity got the best of him, causing him to answer right away.

"Hello," Samir said backing out of the parking spot.

"May I speak with Samir please?" The sultry voice that came from the speakers made Samir's heart skip a beat.

"This is he. Who is this?" There was a slight pause on the other end of the line. Samir glanced at the display to make sure the caller was still there. Seeing the line was still active he opened his mouth to speak, but the woman beat him to it.

"My name is Summer. You may not remember who I am," she chuckled. "But I kind of met you last night at the karaoke bar and wanted to make sure you were okay."

Samir smiled sheepishly because he quietly prayed to thank the woman that saved him from a world of embarrassment. Her voice alone had him at hello and captivated his attention. The thought of how she was able to track him down piqued his mind.

"I'm doing fine. Thank you for what you did last night. You didn't have to call my boy, but you did. I have a few questions for you though. How did you get into my phone and how are you calling me right now?"

"Oh, getting in your phone was the easy part. I just lifted your head and the face recognition did the rest. As far as me calling at this moment, I kind of made a call from your phone to myself. I knew I would be worried sick if I didn't know how you were doing. There's no need to thank me though. My mama and daddy raised a real one and I did what I was supposed to do. There were too many vultures out and you could've been robbed if it had been anyone else getting close to you. Hell, you probably would've gotten taken advantage of."

"You are absolutely right about that," Samir said as Selena's name replaced the number on the display. "Hey, thank you again. I have another call coming through."

"No problem. Enjoy the rest of your day, Samir." Summer ended the call and Samir hit the button to answer Selena's call.

"Hey."

"I saw you called and wanted to hit you back," Selena said dryly. "What's up?"

"Would it be a problem for you to get Sevyn ready for me? I would like to take her with me for about a week. If that's alright with you."

"Samir, that's fine, but shouldn't you be at work?"

Thinking for a moment. Samir wondered if he should indulge in the happenings of his life with Selena. What the hell was he hiding shit for? It wasn't like she could scold him for his actions. When she filed for divorce and had the papers sent to the house, she didn't have a say so in Samir's life. Besides, she had already moved on and was mingling with the next man anyway.

"I got fired a few weeks ago. Now, I want to spend quality time with my favorite girl," Samir said casually.

"You mean to tell me you lost your job and didn't feel the need to tell me," Selena snapped. "You can't help me with our daughter if you don't have steady income coming in, Samir."

"First of all, I don't need to discuss anything with you. Sevyn will always get what she needs from me and that includes time and plenty of love. I've always been a man with a plan. You should know this, Selena. Saving and planning for a rainy day has always been my forte. There's something you have yet to discuss with me, but guess what? It's not my business how you live your life. Make sure you protect my daughter at all costs though."

"Samir, I don't know what you're talking about and Sevyn will always be in good hands with me. I sense a tad bit of animosity coming from you and I don't know why. You are the reason our marriage has come to an end. Be mad at yourself, not me!"

"You're right. I'll be there in about ten minutes to pick up my baby."

"Well, I'm not home. I will call my mama and let her know you're on the way."

Selena hung up and Samir gripped the steering wheel with all his might as he cruised on the highway. The whole divorce thing was eating at him because he still felt Selena should've at least tried to work their marriage out. But like his grandma used to say, *you can't cry over spilled milk. Just keep moving and make do with what you have left.*

Pulling into the driveway of Sandra's house, Samir grabbed the envelope which held the divorce papers and made his way up the stairs. He rang the doorbell and Sandra and Sevyn greeted him at the door. His baby fought trying to get to Samir and that put a huge smile on his face. The gummy grin and the baby squeals almost took him out.

"Hey, Daddy's baby! You're missing me, huh? Daddy misses you too," Samir said, taking Sevyn from her grandmother's arms.

"Samir, it's good to see you," Sandra said, closing the door behind him. "Selena called and told me you were coming by. I'm almost finished getting Sevyn's things together. I should be finished soon."

"I can help you with that to make it easier on you. What do you need me to do?"

"You can start by bathing that little firecracker there. She hasn't been bathed since last night and she has some milk in the crevices of her neck."

"I got you. Come on, little one. Time to rub a dub in the tub."

Sevyn jumped around in Samir's arms and covered him with slobbery kisses. She grabbed his face with both hands and hummed into his jaw. Gathering everything he would need to bathe his daughter, Samir entered the bathroom and turned the water on. Sevyn splashed around as he washed the remnants of the day from her body. Sandra entered the bathroom and captured the moment on camera with her phone.

"That baby has been hollering Dada for the longest and she finally got the opportunity to see the man that makes her little face light up."

"Sandra, whatever is going on between Selena and I have nothing to do with Sevyn. I will always be in her life. She will always have me whenever she needs me. I promise you that."

"I'm so sorry my daughter didn't want to work things out with you. She will come around and realize the mistake you made wasn't quite the reason for her to step away from what the two of you had built together. Relationships today aren't all they're cracked up to be. Selena will have to live and learn."

"No disrespect to Selena, Sandra. But she wanted this divorce and I've given it to her. There's no coming back. I'm only moving forward from this day forward. My only concern is this beautiful little girl right here."

"I understand and don't blame you one bit. You will find love again, Samir. This isn't the last stop for you. I've known you for years and there is a woman out there that will appreciate the love you have to give and the flaws you possess. Build a strong foundation for Sevyn and you won't go wrong in my eyes."

Sandra had all of Sevyn's bags packed with everything she would need for her stay with Samir. There were clothes back at his home, but he would have to go through those items because his baby had grown so much since her mother took her away. As he put the last of the items in his car, Samir went back to grab his daughter from Sandra.

"The envelope on the coffee table is the divorce papers. Make sure Selena gets those. Thanks for looking out for my daughter. I will compensate you next week."

"Samir, get out of my house. I don't need to be paid to take care of my grandbaby. That's what I'm here for. Don't spoil her too much. She seems to act really funky after being with you." Sandra smirked. Giving Sevyn a kiss and big hug, Sandra stepped back so they could leave.

Samir's spirits were lifted to new heights as he strapped his baby in the car seat. He all but ran to the driver's door so he could get home and have his baby girl all to himself. Putting his car in reverse, Samir decided to head to his mother's house first so she could swoon over his baby girl too. Summer's voice echoed in his mind as he drove, but he would think about how to handle that situation at a later date.

Chapter 15

Selena was working when Samir called her about picking Sevyn up. Hearing that he was fired from his job was a surprise because he had been on that job for several years. Him losing his position probably had something to do with the broad he was messing around with. But like he said, it wasn't her business. Samir said something that had her thinking hard about what he meant. Selena did have a secret that she thought was well hidden from his wandering eye, and that was dealing with Frank so soon after leaving her marriage. There was no way he should know about that though.

"I can't wait to get the pictures from this shoot," Amy said, looking over the images on Selena's camera. "My skin is glowing like never before. This baby is bringing out the best in me."

"Pregnancy will do that to many women. I'm glad you trusted me to bring your vision to life," Selena responded as the bell on the door sounded.

Turning to see who was entering, she smiled as Frank walked in her direction with a bouquet of roses. Selena had stayed clear of him after the things she'd learned from Lacy. She wanted to ask him about his wife, but didn't want things to end between them just yet. Frank wore a black tank with a pair of black and red shorts that had his member bouncing against his thigh with ever step he took. Amy's eyes were fixated in the same area when Selena turned to tell her they were finished.

"Ummmm, you can go to the back and change now. We're done here."

"I'm so sorry, Selena. I was distracted for a minute. I didn't mean to be disrespectful, but that is a beautiful sight to see." Amy smiled, walking away.

"Hello, beautiful."

"Frank, how are you so comfortable walking around with all your goods swinging about like a baseball bat?"

He laughed as he leaned in and kissed her cheek. Selena accepted the flowers while blushing from Frank's gesture. He hugged her around the waist and swayed with the music playing in his head while breathing in her sweet scent.

"Hey, this is nature, baby. It's too hot for me to be walking around with my balls balled up accumulating heat. I love to swing freely," he said, hunching his shoulders.

"What are you doing here?" Selena asked.

"I just came through to spend this beautiful day with you. How much longer before you can get out of here?"

"I'm the boss, Frank. I don't punch a clock. Actually, I finished my last session of the day and was going to call it quits after cleaning up this mess."

"So, does that mean I can have you to myself for the rest of the day? Or do you have to spend time with little Sevyn Streeter?"

"Stop calling my baby that," Selena laughed, hitting Frank's muscular bicep. "I'm free to hang. The baby is spending time with her father."

"Well, let's get this shit cleaned up so we can get the hell out of this joint."

Frank and Selena cleaned the studio and Amy had bided her goodbyes while they were still working. Big belly and all, she couldn't keep her eyes off the man Selena was very interested in. Keeping her feelings at bay, she wanted to let things flow as they may without forcing anything. As much as Selena wanted to throw the kitty at Frank, the fact that he had a wife lingered in the back of her mind.

Selena locked up and followed Frank to his car. She didn't mind leaving her vehicle in front of her studio because she had cameras all around the establishment. Sinking into the leather seats of the Mercedes AMG GT, Selena bobbed her head to Kendrick Lamar's *Mr. Morale & the Big Steppers* album. The man was a realist and a prolific poet when it came to his music. There's no way these folks would silence him because he came harder every time, spitting nothing but truth.

"Let me find out you like rap music," Frank said, glancing over at Selena quickly.

"I'm more of an old skool rap girl. The new age music is more about the beat for me. The lyrics are mumble jumble and I can't get with it. We're losing all the legends, but I'll go back in the crate to listen to the shit I can rock with."

"I feel you on that. You seem to rock with Kendrick though."

"I do. He speaks truth and about a lot of things going on in the real world. You know, the shit nobody wants to talk about."

"I wanna see how down you are with the rap game," Frank said, shuffling through his phone while keeping his eye on the road. "If you can rock this song all the way through, I'll give you whatever you want. Deal?"

"Go for it." Selena sat up in her seat waiting for the beat to drop. She looked at Frank with a stank face when the music started.

So you wanna be a gangster, all that shit
Smoke any motherfucker don't even trip
You be hard as hell, take whatever you want
Punk suckas wanna front, they get done

"Nah, you ain't supposed to know that! What you know about Too Short?" Frank laughed. "That one don't count because you cheated. Here's another one."

Selena smiled when the piano started playing and cleared her throat.

His palms are sweaty, knees weak, arms are heavy
There's vomit on his sweater already, mom's spaghetti, he's nervous
But on the surface, he looks calm and ready to drop bombs
But he keeps on forgetting what he wrote down, the whole crowd grows so loud
He opens his mouth, but the words won't come out
He's choking, how?
Everybody's joking now
The clock's run out
Time's up, over blaow

Snap back to reality—

"Okay, okay. You got it," Frank laughed. "You an undercover gangsta. Any woman that can spit Em like that deserves the world. I'm lowkey scared of yo' ass though."

"Just take me to eat then we can go wherever you want to go."

"Say less."

Frank decided on soul food and then headed for his house. Selena was kind of leery going to his home, but she didn't think he would put her in harm's way. They pulled into the driveway of a two-story home that was lavishly put together on the outside. The long driveway seemed as if it was everlasting until he parked in front of the entrance. Frank grabbed the food and got out of the car. Opening the passenger door for Selena, he held her hand and led the way up the stairs.

After entering the code on the keypad, he pushed the door open, allowing her to step in first. Frank's house was beautiful and very homely. From the high ceilings to the bay windows, the scene before Selena was like one from a Paramount movie.

"You have such a beautiful home," Selena said looking around. "Why do you have all this house and you live alone?"

"Who said I live alone? I never told you that, Selena."

Selena was stumped and didn't want to spoil the mood by going further with the conversation. But on the other hand, it was a perfect time to dig into his life and learn the truth. Hayden's words played in her head. *Frank will be straight up with you if you ask.*

"No, you didn't tell me that, but um, tell me about your living arrangements."

"I have no problem with that. I'm married, with no kids. My wife is in the Army and has been abroad for the past year. We have an understanding when it comes to me dealing with other women. She understands a man has needs. Long as I don't fall in love, it's cool for me to mingle a little bit."

Hearing Frank break down the arrangement he and his wife had made Selena feel a kind of way. If she wanted the foolery of sharing, she could've stayed in her marriage. Dealing with someone else's husband wasn't what Selena had in mind. Even though she liked Frank, she didn't want to get too deep with him knowing his wife could pop up at any given time.

"I'm not into any of that, Frank. I just left my marriage because my husband stepped out on me. I like you, but I'm not trying to be involved with someone that has a whole wife. I've been the woman on the other side of cheating. It's not a good feeling at all."

"Selena, I'm not cheating," Frank said, wrapping his arms around her waist. "My wife knows what it is and gave her blessings."

Frank kissed the side of Selena's neck and palmed her ass. The feeling made its way right to her kitty. Her first thought was to request an Uber and leave, but the absence of sex had her melting in his arms. Selena wasn't thinking with her head at that point. She was allowing her pussy to do the talking.

Frank knew he had Selena right where he wanted her. After weeks of communication and dates, it was time for him to test her sweet center to see if she was capable of handling what he had in store. Sliding his hands in the back of her leggings, Frank massaged her folds with his fingers. Selena wet up his palm as he strummed her pearl. Without thought, Frank lifted her against the wall, and she automatically wrapped her legs around his waist.

"Frank, I can't do this," Selena moaned.

Instead of responding, Frank used the wall to help hold Selena while he freed one of her legs from the leggings. In one swift movement, his member was at her entrance and she gasped. Rotating his hips, Frank had her forgetting everything he had said about his wife. Selena threw her love box back at him and rode the wave. She hadn't felt that good since the last time she and Samir had sex. It was so long ago she couldn't remember and had no plans on trying. There was a new pipe layer in her life. She would let him play until it was time to give him back to his rightful owner.

Meesha

Chapter 16

"Hey, Chade. What's good with ya?" Wes asked the minute the call connected.

"All is good, fam. I'm about to be a daddy!"

"What? You done planted yo' seed in my girl? Congratulations! I'm gon' have to call Baylei, because she didn't even tell me."

Chade put the paperwork he was working on to the side and propped his feet on the desk. Wes calling gave him the break he was fighting hard not to take. He was going over an account that a client swore was wrong, but so far, Chade saw that all the numbers were correct. The way things were looking, the card they gave their son was where all the money was being spent. He knew his client was going to be pissed and he would probably end up on the nightly news by morning.

"Lei is still trying to grasp the news herself. We haven't told many about the baby, but in due time. She wants to get confirmation from her doctor first because she only took a test. Once she knows for sure, I'm quite sure she's going to let the world know about it."

"Yeah, that sounds like Baylei. Anyway, one of Donovan's friends there in California is looking for a new financial advisor. I thought of you when he brought it to my attention. Will you be able to help?"

Chade looked around his office and knew he had enough on his plate and wouldn't be able to take the assignment. A light bulb went off in his head and he knew right off back who to pass it on to. Samir was just as good as Chade and he trusted his homie. Plus, he was in need of a gig at the moment.

"Thanks for thinking of me, but my plate is on overload. I can guide you in the direction of my homeboy Samir though. He is nine years in the field and I wouldn't put my name on the line if he wasn't capable of handling the job.

"It's all good. Give me his information so I can pass it along. You know we try to keep shit like this in the family. We don't go outside the circle unless it's necessary. Well, I won't hold you much longer. I have to get this information back, and maybe your boy will be working on a new assignment soon."

"No doubt. I'll talk to you soon."

Chade hung up the phone and glanced at the calendar. In one week, he would be turning thirty-three years old. His life had made a turn for the better and he was actually looking forward to his birthday. Baylei being pregnant was the only present he needed to jump start a new year of life. Chade was so happy that he couldn't hold back telling his mother the news another day. He picked his phone up and dialed his mom and waited for her to answer.

"Hello, son. You always seem to call whenever I'm getting pampered."

Chade could hear the happiness in his mother's tone and it brought a smile to his face. "Maybe I know the precise moment you're out getting more beautiful than you already are. How are you, Ma?"

"I'm good, but I know you're not calling to inquire about me. I can hear it in your voice, you're happy. I'll be sending Baylei a bouquet of roses because she has settled your ass all the way down. I owe her more than that to be honest. All she needs to do know is give me a grandbaby."

"There you go with that mess," Chade laughed. "You've been asking for a grandchild since the day I graduated college and landed the job with the bank."

"And now you're engaged and living with one woman. A respectable woman at that, Chade. It's time for you to be a family man. I already know that baby is going to be beautiful. I had a dream about fish the other night. You know what that means, don't you?"

"What, Chaya is pregnant?" he said, messing with his mother.

"She better not be! That damn girl is out of control in her own way, but she ain't bringing no babies in this house!" Capri didn't play when it came to her baby girl. Chaya may have been twenty-five, but she still lived at home. In Capri's mind, you weren't grown until you had your own.

"Nah, for real, Ma. I was calling to tell you that Baylei found out she's pregnant."

140

"Yes, Lord! Thank you, Jesus! I'm finally getting my grand-baby!" Capri screamed with tears running down her face. The women in the nail shop started clapping and Chade smiled right along with them. "Chade, you don't know how happy you just made me. I've waited to hear those words far too long. How far along is she?"

"We won't know until she goes to the doctor in a couple days. I'll make sure to give all the details soon as I get them."

"Please do. And don't mention the flowers to Baylei. I've changed my mind. She deserves something more extravagant than that. You just made my day."

"I'm glad I could bring a little sunshine into your life. I need to get off here because I have work to do. I love you, mama."

"I love you too, baby. My baby is having a baby! God is good!" Capri said, ending the call.

***

Sevyn was finally down for her nap and Samir could finally shut his eyes while she slept. His daughter was very active and missed him just as much as he'd missed her. Having Sevyn in his home filled in the silence of him being there alone. The way she cried, laughed, or just screamed out of nowhere was like music to his ears. Selena had called via Facetime on many occasions to check on the baby. The conversations were between the two of them as if Samir wasn't even in the room. When Selena was satisfied with seeing Sevyn, she would just end the call.

Samir got comfortable in his bed and tuned in to *Black Ink Crew*. He hadn't been watching the show in a while and wanted to catch up on the happenings. As he enjoyed his show the phone rang and he didn't recognize the number. Samir started not to answer, but then again, he had submitted many applications in the following days.

"Hello."

"Yes, this is Lacy Vick from Vick's Enterprise. I was given your information from Weston King." Samir racked his brain trying to figure out who Weston King was. Then it dawned on him that he was Baylei's boss back in Chicago. "We are looking for a financial advisor and would like to know if you would be able to come in for an interview on Monday."

"Yes. I will definitely be there."

Samir wrote down the information Lacy gave him and thanked her again for considering him. Lying back on the bed, Samir put his hands over his head and finished watching his show. About fifteen minutes later, his phone rang again. It had to be something in the air because he didn't get multiple calls like that. Baylei's name appeared on the screen and he answered quickly.

"Hello. Is everything okay?" Samir asked with concern.

"Yes, everything is good. I'm calling because as you know, Chade's birthday is next week. I'm giving him a surprise dinner party and want you and the guys to get him there without giving my plans away. Can you handle that for me?"

"No, doubt. I'll put the rest of the guys on alert. Just keep me posted and we will definitely be there. You do know Chade hates surprises."

"This is going to be the year he gets over that mess. I'm a girl that's full of surprises, and it doesn't have to be a special occasion for me to do it either. The love I have for Chade is indescribable and I'm here to provide all the peace he needs in his life. He will never have to question my love."

"I hear you, lil mama. I got you though."

"Thank you, and enjoy the rest of your day, Samir."

"You too, Baylei."

Samir got comfortable again and ended up drifting off to sleep. He didn't know how long he'd been asleep, but he was awakened by Sevyn's drool on his cheek. The room was dark except for the luminating glow of the television. Opening one eye, she stuck her thumb right in the middle of his pupil.

"What is it, Daddy's baby?" he asked, rubbing his wounded eye. Sevyn was standing with her little fist wrapped around his shirt as she bounced up and down.

"Dada. Dada. Dada," she said, clapping her hands and before falling backwards. Samir's reflexes were quicker than Spiderman's as he clasped his hand around her little ankle.

"That was a close one. You gotta be careful, baby. I wouldn't hear the end of it from your mama if you kissed that floor."

Samir changed his daughter's diaper and prepared himself to play airplane with her dinner. As he sat Sevyn in the high chair, his phone chimed with a text. Opting to let the person wait while he finished preparing the baby food. Samir sat at the table and gave his daughter a spoonful of rice cereal, mashed spinach, and apple sauce. Grabbing his phone, he opened the texted and read it silently.

(310) 555-0030: Hey Samir, this is Summer. Just wanted to know if you wanted to go out on the town tonight. That is, if you're not tired after work.

Samir smiled while trying to figure out a response. He wouldn't mind going out with Summer and it wouldn't be anything to drop Sevyn off to her mama for a few hours. Sevyn let out a gut-wrenching scream while pounding her little hands on the high chair tray snapping Samir from his thoughts. He laughed when she tossed her sippy cup in his direction.

"You're too young to be bossy. I get it though, you're hungry and Daddy's playing around. Here you go," he said, flying the spoon around over her head.

Giving him a nasty look, Samir stopped trying to make his daughter smile and just fed her. Sevyn was upset and couldn't express herself verbally. Her facial expression told him exactly how she felt. She ate quietly as she rubbed her eyes periodically until every morsel was gone. Samir cleaned Sevyn up and placed her in the bed and surrounded her with pillows before lying down himself. Going back to his phone, he read over the text Summer sent.

Samir: Sorry I'm just getting back with you. I was occupied with my daughter. Far as hitting the town tonight, no can do. I'm on Daddy duty tonight. Maybe sometime in the future we would be able to go out.

(310) 555-0030: It's okay. Your daughter comes first. How old is she?

Samir: She's six months.

(310) 555-0030: Aw, you have a new baby. One day I'll be able to be someone's mommy. What's her name?

Samir: Her name is Sevyn. She was born on the seventh and I love the artist Sevyn Streeter lol.

(310) 555-0030: Sevyn Streeter is the shit! I love it. How are you doing? I could tell you had a lot on your mind while at the bar. I've never seen anyone get wasted like that just because. You don't seem like the type.

Samir thought about how deep he wanted to go with someone he didn't know. He usually kept his personal business to himself because he didn't want to be judge behind his fuck up. Especially talking to another female about the ordeal. He really didn't want to go into detail and was about to skate around the subject when another text came through.

(310) 555-0030: You don't have to talk about it if you don't want to. I know we don't know one another, but when I called around for someone to come get you that night, I called your wife first. She didn't respond, so that's how I called your friend Chade. In my opinion, that was wrong of her. Whether you all are going through something or not, your well-being should've been a priority to her.

Samir: That may be true in the eyes of others. I just don't believe she had an obligation to come to my rescue in my time of need. I put myself in the predicament to be drunk without a way home and I have to live with that.

Samir sent the text and thought about pouring his heart out to the woman that met him and he didn't get the chance to enjoy her company.

Samir: I messed up our marriage by stepping out on my wife. Allowing my feelings to lead me in the direction of bedding another woman was the wrong move to make. I lost everything with the decision I made. My job and my family was the sacrifice I made after doing the things I did out of feeling neglected by my pregnant wife. So, everything that is happening was meant to go down the way it did. I have no problem going out with you, but the way my life is set up at this time, a new relationship isn't something I'm ready for at this time. If anything, I need a friend.

(310) 555-0030: Everyone makes mistakes, Samir. The question is, have you learned from it? I wouldn't try to pursue you in any manner other than friendship. I don't know how long you were married and I would never want to be a rebound woman. Hell, you and your wife may be back together months from now. You never know. I can be the person that keeps your mind off the happenings in your life; as a friend, of course.

Samir: I don't think we will get back together. She is already back out there dating. Plus, I signed the divorce papers she had delivered. I have no more fight in me. She wanted a divorce and I gave it to her. My only concern is my daughter and I'm willing to co-parent. Sevyn will know who her father is. I won't send a check without spending time. My daughter will definitely have active memories with me.

(310) 555-0030: I wish there were more men out there thinking this way. I've seen too many men as of late not being able to accept a woman not wanting to be with them. It breaks my heart that a woman is killed by a man because he has the 'If I can't have her, no one will' mentality. Then there are kids involved and, in some cases, the man takes the woman away from the child and afterward takes his own life. Now, the child has to be raised by family members without experiencing the love of the mother nor father.

Summer was talking real shit and Samir felt every word. There was a time after Selena first stated she wanted a divorce that Samir wanted to strangle her ass. Thoughts of killing her were in the forefront of his mind, but he had to think about how that would've destroyed everything he'd worked hard for. As Summer said, he wouldn't want Sevyn not knowing her mother. She wouldn't have any recollection of Selena if he had carried out his thoughts of killing her. There was no way he would've went out by committing suicide so, he too would've spent the rest of his life behind the wall. That wouldn't have been good for Sevyn either.

Samir's thoughts made him very weary and sleep was the only thing on his mind. He was enjoying the conversation with Summer, but he was overwhelmed with how he had thought about committing murder in the first degree. Glancing down at a sleeping Sevyn, Samir typed out one last text to Summer.

Samir: Thank you for checking on me. I'm going to get some rest before Sevyn decides she wants to play in the wee hours of the morning. I will lock your number in. Goodnight, Summer. I enjoyed our talk.

Samir put his phone on the night stand and draped his arm around his baby girl. He gave her a kiss on the forehead then closed his eyes, letting sleep consume him.

Chapter 17

Selena walked through Target, shopping for necessities that she would need for her new place. Since having lunch with Lacy and Hayden, the two women developed a nice friendship. It came about during a conversation that Selena was looking for an apartment for her and Sevyn because she was tired of her mother questioning her about the decision to divorce Samir. The deed was already done, and there wasn't anyone on earth that would persuade her to reverse it. Her marriage ran its course, now it was over.

Lacy talked with Hayden and they suggested she stop looking for a place. When Lacy came by the house for a girls' day, she took Selena to Vick's Condominiums and showed her around a two-bedroom condo. Selena fell in love the moment she entered. The layout was just what she needed. It was spacious and had more than enough room for her and Sevyn. The dining room was something Selena wouldn't need, but she had a vision of turning it into an office space. Selena had moved in the day before and it felt good to have the freedom of living alone again.

Frank was a huge help to Selena during her move. Without him, she would have had to call professional movers because there was no way she would've called upon Samir. Since the day she gave herself to Frank, Selena fought every waking hour of the day to keep her feelings at bay. The way the man caressed her inner folds made her feel as if she was on cloud nine. For him to have a wife, Frank licked every crevice of her body as if he was an available bachelor. Nothing in the world could convince Selena that he was happily married.

At first, the thought of messing around with a man who was married was out of the question. The thought of another woman having sex with her husband made her say fuck it. She was hurt, so why not place that hurt on another woman as well? Hell, she couldn't be the only female out there in the streets being cheated on. Selena felt as long as his wife didn't know, Frank was free game to get all the goodies. Long as he kept fucking her the way he'd been, they wouldn't have any problems.

Selena walked down the baby aisle and her phone rang. Taking the phone from her purse, she let out a soft sigh. "Hey, Baylei. How's things going?" Selena asked, looking through the pretty outfits on the rack.

"I was calling to see how you've been, since you haven't had time to kick it with us."

"Yeah, I'm sorry about that. Getting back to work has been hard since I've been out so long. Maybe we can plan something for next week. I'll definitely be free."

"That's good to know, because I was calling to invite you to Chade's birthday dinner next Saturday. Please don't try to say you won't be available because you just said you were."

Selena purposely didn't respond because she had already put her foot in her mouth when the conversation started. One thing she knew was, she didn't want to be in the presence of Samir. She didn't know how that would play out since they were in the middle of a divorce. Selena also didn't know how thigs would play out once she walked into the event with Frank on her arm.

"Are you still there?" Baylei asked.

"Yeah, I'm here. Look, Baylei, I don't know if you are aware or not, but Samir and I are no longer together. Chade is his friend, and I don't think it would be wise for me to show up right now. Samir hasn't really spoken on how he feels about us going our separate ways."

"You and Chade have been like family for years. This is a surprise party for his birthday, and I'm quite sure he would love to see you in attendance. It's your call." Selena's phone vibrated in her hand and she looked down and saw a text from Baylei. "I just sent the official invitation to your phone. If you change your mind, show up. I'll talk to you later because I have more calls to make. Enjoy the rest of your afternoon.

Baylei disconnected the call, leaving Selena speechless. To even get invited to attend one of Samir's friend's events had her feeling as if it was a setup of some kind. There was no way she would show up and pretend to have a good time knowing she had hurt the man she made a vow to love and cherish by leaving him.

Selena didn't regret her choice because he put his dick where it didn't belong.

Selena finished her shopping and left the store. She was heading to her mother's house to get some things she had left. Once she got home, Selena had plans to finish Sevyn's room. Her bedroom furniture was delivered earlier that morning and she wanted to finish painting before her baby came home in a few days.

Samir called saying he had an interview on Monday and Selena didn't want anything to stand in the way of him getting employed again. The moment she pulled into her mother's driveway, a feeling overcame her and she didn't know what it was about. Using her key, she walked into the house and her mother met her at the door with a frown on her face.

"Who is Frank, Selena?" Sandra asked.

Stunned that her mother knew about Frank, Selena couldn't do anything except swallow the lump that formed in her throat. "Um, why do you ask?"

"Don't try to answer a question with a question. I asked first and I'm expecting an answer from you."

"I'm grown and it doesn't matter who he is. Now answer my question."

"He came by here looking for you. There must be something going on between y'all if he's coming by here looking for you. Selena, the damn ink ain't even dry on the divorce papers and you got another man in your life." Sandra was preaching to the choir because Selena didn't want to hear what she had to say. "That man looks like he's up to no good. I'd advise you to stay away from him. The only thing he has in store for you is a bad time. Mark my words."

"You don't even know him! All this is coming about because you think Samir is the best thing since sliced bread. His ass wasn't shit and here you stand praising him. Samir can do no wrong and now you want to assume the man that's only a friend is the devil. Get the hell out of here with all that. This is the reason I had to get out of this house with you. I won't sit around while you constantly through shit in my face. If you want Samir in your life so bad, you fuck him!"

Selena stormed to the room she once occupied with her mother on her heels. Sandra was boiling from the way her daughter had spoken to her and she wasn't about to allow her to disrespect her in the home she paid the bills in. The only thing she was trying to get her daughter to understand was she didn't need a man to complete her.

"You're mad at the wrong person. You should be mad at yourself. If you want another man to dog you out, you may as well make things right with your husband. At least you know what he's about. This new cat is going to break your heart in a million pieces. It wouldn't surprise me if he was hiding a wife or the mother of his children."

Sandra said the key words and caused Selena's spine to stiffen. Her mother knew nothing about Frank's wife, but she spoke that shit like she had the inside scoop. Selena wanted to say something, but her mother was on a roll.

"You may not agree with the things I say, but you will respect me in my home. I would never say anything that's not of the better good when it comes to you, Selena. One thing I would never do is try to make you live your life the way I would like, but I can smell a bad outcome a mile away. This man is not the one for you. Even if you don't want anything to do with Samir, at least find yourself and learn to love yourself before jumping into something new."

"Mama, I know you mean well. But I'm a mother now and I do believe I can make my own decisions. You're going to have to let me live my life the way I see fit. I appreciate you trying to school me, but I don't need your advice on any of my relationships. If you had used your own advice, maybe you wouldn't be in this house alone, hoping and praying a man that never loved you reappeared."

Selena knew the minute the words left her mouth she was wrong. Bringing her parents relationship into their disagreement was fucked up and she owed her mother an apology. Selena turned with a softened heart and tears in her eyes."

"I'm so sorry—"

"Never apologize for speaking your truth. When that man breaks your heart in two, my door will be open. Don't hesitate to come to me. I will always be here for you when you need me." With that, Sandra walked out of the doorway and a few seconds later her bedroom door shook the house as she slammed it shut. Selena let the tears fall as she gather her belongings and left her mother's home. Driving home in silence with the conversation with her mother playing repeatedly in her head, Selena felt as if she lost everything in life when her mother walked away from her.

In her mind, Sandra wanted her to settle for a man that cheated. She didn't want to deal with that. Instead, she was falling for a man that had a wife and might turn his back on Selena when she came back from wherever she was. Selena thought dealing with Frank was easier than being locked in a marriage where the trust was gone. At least with Frank, he was honest about his marital status and she wasn't obligated to be with him. Samir had an obligation to be faithful and he couldn't even do that. Selena was ready to go out there and be free. Whatever that was, she would find out on her new journey.

***

Frank was at Selena's home, waiting for her to come through the door. He'd stopped by her mother's thinking she would be there so they could go to her condo together since he was in the neighborhood. Meeting her mother on the front porch was no walk in the park. The woman looked upon him as if he was a thief in the night. Frank knew all about Selena's ex and how she had filed for divorce, but what did that have to do with him? Selena's mother spoke to him in the nastiest tone and he thanked her for whatever reason and left.

He decided to use the key he never returned after arranging the furniture in her new place. He took it upon himself to finished painting her daughter's bedroom so she wouldn't have to. The pink and white color scheme was beautiful and he loved the way it turned out. After finishing his task, he went into the kitchen to whip something up for them to eat. Frank found steak, broccoli and pota-toes to make a delectable dish. The aroma of the food had his taste-buds excited as he took the wine from the freezer before setting the table for two.

Selena entered her home and looked around in confusion. She didn't start anything for dinner before she left so, her thoughts were, what the hell was smelling so good? Walking into the kitchen, she looked around at the table and smiled when Frank wrapped his arms around her waist then kissed her neck.

"Welcome home, beautiful," he said, leading Selena to the ta-ble. He pulled the chair out for her and proceeded to prepare their plates. "I went by your mom's looking for you."

"Yeah, about that. What actually happened today, Frank?"

Placing the plates on the table, Frank sat down across from Selena. "Your mother gave me attitude the moment she opened the door. The only thing I did was introduce myself and asked if you were there. Nothing else was said, so I thanked her and got back in my car."

Selena believed everything Frank said. Her mother was defi-nitely in her feelings about a strange man coming to see her daugh-ter. Frank had picked her up from there plenty of times, but Selena never gave him a chance to come to the door. She could only imag-ine the look on her mother's face. It really didn't matter because she had already addressed the situation. There was no need to go into it any further.

"Anyway, how was your day? Did you go into the shop at all?" Selena asked as she poured steak sauce on the meat in front of her. "Thank you for making dinner."

"You're quite welcome. I went in for a little while, then I de-cided to come over to give you a hand with lil mama's bedroom."

"I'm so sorry for messing up your plans. You can come over tomorrow and we can finish the room."

"No need, hun. I've already completed that task and then cooked. Now enjoy your meal so I can have you for dessert."

Selena and Frank enjoyed each other's company while eating, then they cleaned the kitchen and washed the dishes together. Frank

152

took her by the hand and led the way to Sevyn's bedroom. When they entered the room, Selena's eyes lit up at the sight of the room. Frank had painted the room better than she ever could and she loved it.

"Frank, this is so beautiful. I didn't know you knew how to write in calligraphy! The way Sevyn's name is displayed with the princess theme is amazing."

Frank smiled and without thought, Selena kissed him fully on the lips. He slipped his tongue in her mouth and they had a make out session right in the middle of the baby's room. When Frank picked Selena up off her feet and walked her down the hall, she knew the fun was just beginning and looked forward to whatever he had in store.

Meesha

Chapter 18

Samir showed up to the address Lacy Vick provided and made sure he dressed in his best for the interview. Running his hand down the front of his grey suit jacket, Samir looked down and made sure everything down to his shoes were good. With his briefcase with his resumé and other important documents inside, he made his way to the front desk.

"Good morning, Sir. How may I help you?" the young lady behind the desk asked.

"My name is Samir Jamison. I'm here to see Lacy Vick. I have an interview at ten."

"Oh, Mr. Jamison. Mrs. Vick has been waiting for your arrival. Follow me this way and good luck."

Samir was led to the back of the establishment and straight to an office door. The young lady rapped on the door three times, then a voice on the other side invited them inside. Sitting behind the desk was a beautiful woman that didn't look a day over twenty. There was no way she could be the boss of this massive company. Samir had heard about Vick's Security, and it was a lucrative business for the elite crowd.

"Mr. Jamison, it's nice to finally put a face to the name. Take a seat. We will begin the moment my husband gets off a very important call. I'm Lacy, by the way," she said, rising from her seat with her hand held out.

Samir shook her hand and sat in the seat in front of her desk. He looked around the room, admiring the décor. Mrs. Vick was typing away on her computer, periodically glancing up at him with a slight smile. After placing his resumé on the desk, Samir took the opportunity to text Summer to see how she was doing while he waited. Before he could type out the message, the door to the office opened. Glancing up from his phone, Samir jumped to his feet soon as he saw the man standing before him.

"This has got to be a fuckin' joke. What type of bullshit are you on?" Samir asked with his fists clenched at his side.

"Samir, calm down," Hayden said, closing the door.

"Don't use my name like you know me, muthafucka! I don't know what type of games you're playing, but I don't want any parts of it. What makes you think I would want to do business with you and you're fucking my wife?"

Lacy looked over at Hayden with a questionable expression. She knew for a fact her husband wasn't sleeping with anyone's wife because he knew she didn't play that shit. Lacy tried to figure out why the man in front of her was so angry, then it dawned on her. The man standing in the middle of her office was Selena's husband. She had no idea he didn't know who he was interviewing with and Hayden was the last person he wanted to see after their altercation at the sports bar.

Hayden walked toward Samir with his hands up. "Look, like I tried to explain to you the day we met, Selena and I have nothing going on. She ran into the back of my car. When you walked into the sports bar that day, she was so sad and I was there to listen to her. Lacy is my wife. She knows all about that day."

"How the fuck did you get my information? I don't need a job that bad to work for the muthafucka that is interested in my wife. Do you know she filed for divorce because of your ass?" Samir sneered.

"No, she filed for divorce because of your infidelities. Own up to that shit, Samir," Hayden said truthfully. "As far as how I got your information, I called a friend to see if they knew of someone that could help me with my finances and your name came back with damn good references. Regardless of what you're thinking, I need your business expertise. Selena is a good friend of my wife and I, nothing more. Samir, you and I got off on the wrong foot and I would like to reintroduce myself. I am Hayden Vick, and I would love to work with you."

Samir still didn't let his guard down after Hayden's explanation because he didn't believe a word he'd said. He was the man Samir walked up on holding his wife's hand in public and gazing in her eyes. There was chemistry between them, and Samir wasn't about to allow Hayden to lie in his face.

"That's sounds good, bro, but you of all people know that's a lie. The way you were looking at my wife told me everything I needed to know."

"Samir, I know you are upset," Lacy said softly. "Hayden isn't the man Selena is dating. I have become a good friend to your wife. Trust me, you're accusing the wrong man. I'm not permitted to tell you *who* the guy is that's courting her, but I would put my life on the line by telling you it's not my husband. Now, I reached out to you after Weston King sent me your information and told me you were highly recommended by a Chade Oliver. If you want the job, it's yours."

Samir couldn't stand in the office another minute while the two played in his face surrounding his wife. He'd seen things unfold right before his eyes and wasn't buying anything Hayden and his wife said. Snatching his briefcase off the floor, he brushed past Hayden and left without another word.

"Hayden, we need to get him back in here," Lacy said as she handed her husband a piece of paper. "He's good at what he does and, in my heart, I believe we owe him this position."

Looking over the papers, Hayden looked up at his wife. "If you want him on the team, I'll try my best to get him back. But he will have to leave the bullshit outside the door. I've never pled my innocence to another man like that a day in my life. It was hard for me to deescalate the situation professionally. The old me would've just beat his ass and been done with it."

Leaving the office, Hayden went searching for Samir. When he got to the parking lot, he didn't see any signs of him. Samir would hear from the Vick's again because there was money to be made, and Samir deserved a second chance at happiness.

***

Samir stormed into Chade's workplace without stopping at the desk to see if he was available. Knocking on Chade's office door, he twisted the knob once he was summoned to enter. Chade was shocked to see his friend breathing like a raging bull so early in the morning. It could only be one thing, or should he say, one person. Selena.

"Why the hell would you recommend me to work with someone that's dealing with my wife?" Samir smacked his palms on the desk right in front of Chade.

"Yo! What the fuck is your problem, man? You know not to come at me with that kind of bullshit! Now, calm the fuck down and tell me what you're talking about, because I'm clueless."

Samir remained standing as he glared at his long-time friend. As of late, he felt there were so many people out to ruin him and he never imagined out of everyone his boy would be one of them. Yeah, Samir was out of work, but he wasn't in desperate need of a job that bad to work for a man that was exploring his wife's body the way he had.

"That nigga you recommended me to interview with is the same man that was in the restaurant with Selena! Before you give my name to anyone, Chade, know who the fuck you're dealing with! His name is Hayden Vick and I will *not* work with his ass." Samir was pissed off, and Chade understood why after he explained.

"I didn't know who the interview was with because Wes called me for a favor. Instead of taking him up on the job, I passed it along to you because you're out of work. I didn't ask about the details of the position. I knew I couldn't do it. The first person I thought of was you. Now, if I was wrong for trying to put you on, sue me, but what you not gon' do is come at me like I'm some type of shady muthafucka. You and Selena's issues has nothing to do with me. If you allow this shit to stop your money, you stupid."

"I'm not working alongside someone that's banging my wife!"

"Did he admit to sleeping with Selena, Samir?"

"Nah, the nigga denied the shit and so did his wife. He claims what he told me at the sports bar was the truth. His wife, Lacy, said she would bet her life that her husband wasn't sleeping with Selena. She also said she wasn't permitted to tell me who was either."

"Samir, that right there should've let you know that man isn't the one sleeping with Selena. Obviously, he and his wife are cool with Selena on some level. They know exactly who she is dealing with, but it's not their business to reveal who that person is. Had you listened to what was being said instead of what you wanted to hear, you would've peeped the shit the same way I just did," Chade shook his head in disappointment. "Answer me this. Why are you so worried about who the hell Selena fucking with anyway? She filed for divorce and you signed the muthafuckin' papers, Usher. Who she is spending time with ain't got nothing to do with you, man. Concentrate on getting your life back on track. Obtain a job and move on, like she is doing. I'm not telling you to go fall in love or no shit like that. Go out and at least get some pussy, because your balls are too tight around this bitch," Chade said, looking down at his vibrating phone.

"Yeah, babe." Chade listened as Baylei talked and looked up at Samir. He shook his head continuously as he took in everything his fiancée was saying to him. "Well, I'll talk to you later at home because Samir is here. I love you, and this too shall pass." Chade ended the call and folded his hands together as he leaned forward. "As you could probably tell, that was Baylei. She got a call from Wes asking about your accusations against Hayden. I'm going to call and let him know that Baylei had nothing to do with that interaction and he should've contacted me. Anyway, according to Baylei, Hayden isn't the man that's dealing with Selena. She ran into Selena a few weeks back and saw her with a man. They talked for a few and exchanged numbers."

"Well, who the hell is he?" Samir asked.

"Unfortunately, she, too, said she wasn't getting involved in y'all situation and wasn't willing to drop a name. Again, Samir, go out and enjoy life. Sitting around wondering who and what Selena is doing is going to drive you up the wall. You're going to find yourself sitting in the bar again drunk out of your mind because you are too engulfed in some shit that no longer concerns you. Selena wanted out of the marriage, let her go!"

Samir felt like a fool the way he acted in the Vick's establishment. At the time, he didn't know that Hayden wasn't the man Selena was dating, but now he knew different. Even though Hayden and his wife stressed that to him plenty of times, his emotions didn't allow him to take heed. Chade was right. Samir needed to let Selena go and focus on taking care of his daughter and getting his life together. He may have messed up a great opportunity, but that wasn't going to stop him from striving.

Chapter 19

Baylei was running around trying to get last minute things done before heading to the venue. The party planner did a great job setting up. The pictures she sent were incredible, and Baylei approved. Toni and Jordyn were already there to oversee the caterers, so Baylei just needed to get there before the guests started to arrive. Not only did she plan the surprise dinner, she also had a few more surprises for the love of her life.

Adorning herself in a sequined black mini dress that sparkled in silver and green, her black Louboutin's had her standing like a stallion. Baylei turned side to side in the mirror because she wanted to make sure her stomach wasn't seen in the dress. She had gone to the doctor and confirmed she was definitely pregnant. To her and Chade's surprise, she was already seventeen weeks, and it didn't look like she was pregnant at all. It was a matter of time before the world would be able to tell she was expecting, but her friends and family would find out that night.

Chade didn't know the gender of their child, and that was going to be one of his many surprises from Baylei. She had gone over and beyond for his day and she couldn't wait to see the joy she would bring to him. As she grabbed her clutch and keys, Baylei passed the mirror once more and ran her hand down the front of her dress. The smoky look she went with made her eyes look exotic as hell. Her nude lip set the entire beat off and Baylei loved it.

Her phone rang in her hand and she already knew who was on the end. "I'm leaving out now. I'll be there in twenty."

"Baylei, the guests are already starting to arrive. Capri and Chaya are here. What do you want me to do with them?" Toni asked.

"Allow them to help with whatever needs to be set up. Samir is supposed to have Chade there by seven, so make sure they are out of sight by the time he arrives. I will be there before then, but just in case. Did they deliver the cake already?"

"Yes, I set in out on the table and the buffet is set up as well," Toni confirmed. "You did your thang with this spread, friend. I can't wait to dig into the lobster and crab cakes. One thing I've noticed, this menu is all about your ass," she laughed. "This is supposed to be Chade's night and you worried about self."

"Shut up! Chade appreciates anything I do and that includes my food choices," Baylei retorted as she set the alarm and descended the steps to her car. "I'll see you in a few. I love you and thanks for always being there for me."

"Girl, boo. I love you too."

Baylei cruised through traffic and rocked with Jill Scott the entire way to the venue. Pulling around back, she parked in a spot where Chade wouldn't be able to notice her car and got out. As she walked around to the front of the venue, her phone chimed.

Samir: We'll be there in thirty minutes. This dude is asking so many questions about Ahmad's company dinner party and getting on my nerves. He's clean as a whistle though. You did good, sis.

Baylei: Thank you so much. He has no clue, I hope. I planned this on a Friday because his birthday is actually Sunday and I made imaginary reservations that he knows of for that day. Keep the charade going and get him here.

Samir: I know when that nigga's birthday is, Baylei. You're the new kid on the block *wink emoji*

Baylei: Hush up, fool. I'll see y'all when you get here.

When Baylei stepped foot into the building, the pictures did no justice to what she was seeing in front of her. The silver and black decorations were just what she'd envisioned. Toni walked in her direction in a stunning black floor length dress with a high split on the left side. The heels she wore had her standing tall with confidence and her breasts were standing out for the world to see.

"You are beautiful," Baylei said, hugging her friend. "Everything is perfect!"

"You're not looking bad yourself. I'm loving that dress and those legs! Baby, Chade's jaw is going to hit the floor. Baylei, you out did yourself with this one. If that man ain't already knocked you up, you getting pregnant tonight!"

Baylei blushed because she knew her friend was correct. She hadn't disclosed the news of her pregnancy to either one of her friends, and she almost let the cat out the bag. Toni and Jordyn were going to be highly upset finding out with everyone else, but that's just the way the cookie would crumble. Spotting Chade's mother and sister, Baylei excused herself and made her way over.

"Baylei, you look terrific!" Capri walked toward her daughter-in-law with opened arms. "Congratulations on the new edition," she whispered as she hugged Baylei. "Your secret is safe with me."

"Thank you. I'm going to reveal the gender later tonight. Chade doesn't even know what we're having."

"You know the gender already?" Capri asked, looking Baylei over from head to toe. "You don't look pregnant at all."

"Yes, I'm seventeen weeks. Soon as I make this announcement, I'm going to blow up like a beach ball," Baylei laughed. "It's good seeing you and I'm glad you were able to make it here today. Hey Chaya, how you been?"

"I'm good. Can never miss out on celebrating my brother. Aye, Baylei, tell me how you got Chade to stop chasing every skirt that he passed? No one was ever able to pulled that rabbit out of the hat before."

Baylei laughed because hearing his sister say that only swelled her chest up more for being the one to catch a big fish. "I didn't get him to do anything. To be honest, Chade needed a woman that was worthy of settling down for. All the women before me didn't have the ability to hold shit down, talk to Chade in a manner which touched his heart, and leave all the bullshit at the door. Plus, I came to the table with more than pussy. Excuse my language, Miss Capri."

"Don't worry about the words you used because I heard nothing but truth. The others didn't step their game up and you did just that and turned my son's heart into mush. I have never seen him love anyone the way that he loves you."

"I try to give him all the love he brings to me in return. We laugh, communicate, and keep each other in the loop of everything between us. I wouldn't want to learn this thing called love with anyone else." Baylei smiled. "Chade should be here any minute and you two are one of my big surprises. I'll keep you posted on his arrival. I have to go greet some of the other guests.

Baylei made her way around the room and spotted Selena standing along the wall with the man she called Frank. Things were about to get real because seeing Selena with another man knowing Samir was going to be in attendance could turn out bad. When Baylei invited her, she wasn't expecting the woman to bring a date. Walking in the direction Selena stood, Baylei applied a fake smile as she approached the pair.

"Hey, Selena," she said, looking between the two of them. "Um, can I talk to you for a minute?"

Selena whispered something to her date and followed Baylei into a far corner. They waved to a few people they knew as Baylei was hugged along the way. Once they were alone, Baylei cleared her throat before speaking.

"Um, when I invited you to this event, I didn't expect you to bring someone else along. I don't know the extent of what is going on between you and Samir, but I know for a fact seeing you with someone else isn't going to go very well."

"Baylei, I understand your concern, but Samir has no say so in who I interact with. Frank is here with me because I didn't want to come alone. If it's a problem on his end and you think things will be awkward, I will leave right now. What I won't do is allow that man to dictate my life when we're not together. The reason behind our separation is because of something Samir has done. That's all on him; not me."

Baylei's phone chimed and there was a text from Samir alerting her of their arrival. There was no time for Selena to leave because whether she stayed or not, there may be an altercation between the two regardless. She responded quickly and turned her attention back to Selena.

"You don't have to leave, but know this; Samir is about to enter the building and I don't want no shit. I will talk to him and suggest he leave all that shit for another day. Enjoy yourself, Selena, and thanks for coming."

Baylei walked across the room, grabbed the mic, and informed everyone to gather around the entrance. She, Capri, Chaya, Jordyn, and Toni stood in the front of the crowd. The turnout was great, and her fiancé was going to be in for the surprise of his life. Nodding her head as she saw Sanji leading the pack, the DJ started music for India Arie's "Steady Love". As soon as the doors opened, and Chade entered looking like he stepped off the cover of a magazine, everyone screamed Surprise!

Chade stopped in his tracks and looked around the room with glassy eyes. When his gaze landed on his mother, the waterworks came crashing down. She rushed into his arms and he hugged her tightly before summoning Baylei to join them.

"Thank you so much, beautiful. You get a pass because you didn't know how much I hate surprises. Those other knuckleheads are going to hear my mouth because they pulled the wool over my eyes. Only because of you." Chade kissed Baylei deeply making her forget there was a roomful of people surrounding them.

He released Baylei and picked his little sister up and swung her around. She giggled like a schoolgirl because in Chade's mind, his sister would forever be his little baby. Baylei was so caught up in her man that she forgot all about warning Samir about Selena and her date. By the time she realized, Samir was walking across the room.

"Chade, go stop him. I don't want any trouble." Baylei said, pointing in the direction Samir was headed.

Chade and Sanji were on Samir in a millisecond. They were standing in the middle of the room, trying their best to prevent their friend from causing a scene. Baylei walked up to them and caught the end of Samir's rant.

"How could she come in here parading around with another nigga? That's disrespectful as hell," Samir snapped looking straight at Selena.

"What did I tell you the other day, brah? Move the fuck on," Chade said, grabbing Samir by the shoulder. "So what she's here with someone else? Act like that shit isn't fazing you. Long as you're huffing and puffing by seeing that shit, the wetter her panties is getting for that nigga. The cat looks shiesty than a muthafucka anyway. He's not with her for the long haul. I know his kind."

"I'm cool. Tonight, is about you. Let's turn up for your day," Samir said, giving Chade a brotherly hug. "Yo DJ, run that shit back!"

The way that he looks at me when he holds my hand
He wants everyone to know I'm his woman and he is my man
We talk about everything; he's got nothing to hide
He's not afraid of his feelings, he's not a slave to his pride

Chade swayed in Baylei's arms as she sang off key in his ear. He laughed, but loved every minute of her rendition of the song. The lyrics described the way he felt about her to the T, and he would forever provide the steady love she has been seeking long before meeting him in St. Thomas. Everybody before him fucked up royally when they let the gem in his arms get away.

Everyone sat at their assigned tables after filling their plates to the brim with the delicious food. The DJ put the music on auto play so he could get his grub on as well. Chade was having the time of his life with his family and friends. He would've been content with it only being he and Baylei, but his woman had other plans.

"When are you going to open your gifts?" his mother asked as she sipped from her flute of champagne.

"Gifts? I know damn well y'all didn't buy me anything."

"Boy, please. You always get gifts from me on our day. Of course, I bought you something."

Baylei rose from her seat and went to the wrapped boxes on the table. While standing with her back turned she sent out a quick text and smiled before making her way back to Chade. There were only a few gifts and plenty of envelopes for the birthday boy.

"This is mine, baby. Open it first," Capri said happily.

Chade opened the small box and removed a Cuban linked chain with a diamond encrusted cross pendant. He thanked his mother with a hug and a big kiss. The next box was from Baylei. She studied him so well that she went out and bought him a pair of monogrammed diamond cufflinks with the letters 'CO' on them. Chade

166

gave Baylei a more passionate kiss while thanking her with every peck. She didn't have to get him anything else because all he wanted was her.

Baylei pulled away and went to the mic as her phone buzzed in her hand. She sent another text and cleared her throat. Cueing Jordyn to start the slide show, she got the attention of everyone in the room. As the pictures of she and Chade strolled across the screen, Baylei started speaking to the crowd.

"I want to send a special happy birthday to the man that chose me to be his forever lady. You have touched my heart and soul in so many ways and it's only been six months. I can only imagine what you can do for me in a lifetime."

Baylei turned toward the door as Wes entered the building. She smiled and brought her attention back to what she was saying.

"The joy you have brought into my life can't be beat. You have given me everything I've always wanted in my adult life and that is true love. As you already know, but I want to share with everyone else, I will be giving you something that Ms. Capri has been asking you for damn neat all your life." Everyone laughed. "So, ladies and gentleman, I would like for you all to know that Chade and I are expecting our first child in five months!"

A picture of Chade and Baylei appeared on the screen with a sign that read "We're pregnant! The surprise is on you!" Everyone cheered loudly and Toni and Jordyn raced to Baylei, smothering her with hugs and kisses. Toni kept looking at her stomach, shaking her head.

"You can't be four months pregnant! Where is your belly, Lei? You are wearing the fuck outta that dress and it doesn't scream I'm pregnant."

"Forget all that. Why are we just hearing this with everybody else?" Jordyn questioned.

"Don't take it personal. I wanted everyone to appear surprised because we hadn't told Capri as of yet. I just found out tonight, she already knew." Baylei playfully rolled her eyes.

"Well, what are you having?" Toni asked.

"Y'all about to find out now. Chade doesn't even know and I have the best present that's going to knock him off his feet." She laughed as she placed the microphone back to her mouth. "Chade, baby. I need you and all of your guests to meet me out front. I have one more surprise for you."

"What are you up to, woman?" Chade asked as Baylei grasped his hand in hers.

Leading him outside, she whispered, "You'll see."

When everyone was out of the building, a blacked out Brabus Mercedes Maybach GL5800 rolled into the parking lot and stopped right in front of Chade. The door opened just enough and Donovan stepped out in an all-black suit with a pair of sunglasses over his eyes. Chade and every male behind him whistled loudly.

"Damn, Donovan. That muthafucka is nice," Chade said, walking around the truck. "This how Customs by Dap got you rolling? I want in, fam."

Dap laughed, shaking his head. "Nah, brah, this all you. Happy birthday, Mr. Lover Man," Dap said, giving Chade a brotherly hug.

"Aw, hell nawl! I can't accept this from you," Chade screeched.

"Good thing it's not from me. You better hold on to her, Chade. Baylei is a keeper, man," Donovan said, handing him the keys.

Chade understood Baylei had money, but she was very careful with how she spent it. For her to spend a grip on a truck of this magnitude did something to him. Hell, he didn't want to accept it from her either, but he wasn't going to spoil the moment for her. Baylei walked over and hugged Chade.

"Happy birthday again, Mr. Oliver. Don't say a word; you deserve every bit of this. Now, get in the car and check out your new ride."

"You're definitely tooting that azz in the air when we get home," Chade said, pecking her on the lips.

He opened the door and inspected the black leather interior. Baylei had custom blue stitching in the headrests that read 'C. Oliver'. The shit was smooth as hell and Chade loved it. Noticing a box on the passenger seat, he looked back at Baylei and she nodded her head. Sitting in the driver seat, Chade reached over and opened the box. Inside was a white onesie with blue lettering. He unfolded the material and read what it said.

"What's up, Big Homie? My name is Chade Oliver Jr. but you can call me Son."

Tears flowed down Chade's face and there was nothing he could do to stop them. He placed his head on the steering wheel and cried like a baby. Capri became alarmed and made her way to the truck.

"You okay, baby?"

Wiping his face, Chade got out holding the onesie. "Yeah, I'm good. We're having a boy, y'all! I got a muthafuckin' junior on the way!"

Meesha

Chapter 20

Selena followed the crowd to the door as Baylei instructed. As she walked, she noticed Frank wasn't beside her and turned to see where he was. He was so engulfed in his phone that he didn't even realize she had walked back to him.

"Are you coming outside with everyone else?" Selena asked.

Frank's eyes shifted around the venue before landing on Selena. "I have to go. Will you be able to catch a ride from here? I'm sorry." Frank sped to the door as he talked.

"No, we can leave together. You can just drop me back off at home."

"It's not that simple. There's something I have to do and it's urgent," he said, tapping away on his phone. A few seconds later, a notification appeared on Selena's phone. She pulled the device from her phone and saw a cash deposit for one hundred fifty dollars that Frank deposited into her account.

"What is that for?" Selena asked.

"For you to get an Uber home. I have to go."

Selena followed Frank out of the venue and walked behind him to his car. The cheers around her weren't very festive for Selena. The only thing she was worried about was Frank's quick exit and the way he was brushing her off. As they neared his luxury car, Frank's strides all but stopped. The woman that walked toward him was beautiful. Her body was lean, muscular, and in tip top shape as if she worked out on a daily. The cropped top showed off her toned abs and black leggings captured every curve of her sculpted legs.

"Hello, Frank." She smiled.

"Payton, welcome home baby." He smiled as he gathered her in his arms kissing her vigorously on her lips.

Selena looked around to make sure no one saw what was happening. She had been cozying up with Frank the entire night and gloated at the sight of seeing Samir seething across the room. Now, here she stood watching her date give another woman public affection. Selena knew Frank had a wife, but seeing her in the flesh did something to her mentally. She always told herself when his wife showed up, she would walk away gracefully. At the moment, that wasn't something she wanted to do anymore.

"How did you know where I was?"

"Frank, you are my husband. I know your every move. Just because I haven't been in the States, doesn't mean the location sharing stops. I see you've been pretty busy for the past thirty or so days," Payton said, glancing at Selena. "She's pretty. Does she know?"

"She knows I'm married and that I have permission to see others while you're away."

Selena was growing angrier as the seconds ticked away. The way they talked as if she wasn't there only pissed her off more. She stepped closer to Frank, resting her hand on his forearm.

"I would appreciate if you would talk directly to me and not act like I'm not standing here."

Payton stepped back out of Frank's hug and stared at Selena's hand. She smiled wickedly as she licked her lips. Looking Selena over, she placed her right hand on her hip and placed her left hand against her chin. The diamond on her ring finger was big enough for everyone to see on the other side of the lot.

"What's her name, Frank?"

"My name is Selena. You must be his wife."

"Yes, I am his wife. With you knowing he has one of those, tell me, why are you being so bitter?" Payton quizzed.

"I'm not bitter at all. I mean, you have been gone for what, over a year? I've kept your husband company for—"

"Three weeks and two muthafuckin' days. I've been around for fifteen years. There's not a pussy out here that could take my husband from me. See, me and my husband have an agreement for when I'm gone. He plays and don't get attached, and then when I come home, we all play together. The door is open for you to enter, Selena. Frank knows how I like my women. You are a beauty, and I bet you taste good too. What do you say?"

"Ask your husband if I taste good," Selena sneered.

Payton laughed heartily before responding to Selena's statement. "Frank knows better than to put his mouth on any cat other than mine. Eating pussy is my job, baby. Are you in or not? I mean, you have been spending a lot of time with my husband and your attitude lets me know you're not eager to let him go. You don't have to walk away. I've given you an open invitation."

Selena was pissed because Frank only snuggled closer to his wife as he looked at her seductively awaiting a response. She took a step back, shaking her head.

"Fuck you, Frank," she said as she turned and headed back inside of the venue. Payton and Frank stood watching Selena retreat into the building.

"She'll be calling again, Kitten. Selena loved this dick and she won't be able to live without it."

"I hope so, because I need to see what she's working with between her legs. Let's go home. I have an itch that needs to be scratched."

Selena went straight to the bar and ordered a double shot of Hennessey. Gulping down the drink she ordered another as she grooved to the music. Hearing someone walk up to the bar, Selena didn't bother looking over to see who had joined her. The person whispered the order to the bartender and Selena thought that was strange so she looked over to see who was being secretive. To her surprise, it was Samir.

"You wanna talk about it?" he asked, sitting down.

"Samir, if you want to come over here talking shit, you can just go."

"I'm not even on that, Selena. I truly want to know if you're alright. The way that nigga played you out there—"

"Mind the business that pays you, Samir. I'm no longer your concern and you don't know wat happened between us," Selena said

"I know he chose that woman over yo' ass because you are in here drinking like a fish and he is probably on his way home to break her back. Selena, I know you're done with me and I've come to terms with that."

"Well, why were you about to come over with the bullshit earlier? I saw Chade and Sanji pulling you back," Selena scoffed.

"It is hard for me to see you with another man," Samir laughed lowly. "My feelings aren't as easy to turn off as yours. It took no time for you to move around and look where that got you. Be careful out here, Selena. You are worthy and deserves to be loved fully. I want you to know I'm sorry for doing you the way I did. I'm here for you and Sevyn whenever you need me."

"I don't need you to be there for me. You are doing a great job with Sevyn and that's all I need from you. Me and you are a done deal, Samir. Enjoy your life and good luck on your job search."

Selena pulled out her phone to request an Uber. Samir glanced over and saw what she was doing and stood from his seat. He pulled his keys from his pocket and placed his hand over her phone to stop her from continuing.

"You don't have to do that. I'll take you home, Selena. Come on, let's go." Samir led Selena toward the door and he stopped to talk to Chade. "I'll be back, bro. I'm going to take Selena to the crib."

"What happened to the dude she was with?"

"A bitch showed up and they had words. His punk ass ended up leaving with the other woman and Selena was sitting at the bar drinking her life away."

"If you don't return, that's cool. I appreciate you for helping out with all of this. Thank you, brah."

"No problem. Aye, what did you do with all of those envelopes? There's money in those muthafuckas. At least in mine there is," Samir stated.

"Oh shit! I didn't think about that shit. I left them on the table," Chade said rushing to the table where he was sitting. "Whew, good thing I have trustworthy muthafuckas around me. Back in the day, that shit would've grown legs and walked right on out of here. Good looking."

"A'ight, I'll catch you when I get back. The party will be in full swing by then."

"Indeed. Don't fall in that gushy shit and fuck your mind up all over again," Chade laughed.

"Nah, that's not happenin'. Selena is through with my black ass. Let me get out of here before her ass gets an Uber."

Selena was waiting outside until Samir emerged out of the building. They walked quietly to his car and he went to open the door for her and she smacked his hand in return. Instead of saying anything, Samir walked to the other side and got in his car. Pulling out of the lot, Samir headed in the direction of her mother's house.

"Um, do you know where you're taking me?"

"Yeah, to your mother's house," Samir shot back.

"I don't live there anymore."

Selena gave him her address and Samir knew the area. It wasn't too far away from her studio. He didn't ask any questions and turned the radio on to drown out the silence inside of the car. Samir pulled to the curb about fifteen minutes later and Selena jumped out of the car without saying a word. He waited until she was safely inside the building and pulled off as he made a beeline back to the party.

Meesha

Chapter 21

Baylei helped Chade celebrate his birthday like a king. She took everyone's breath away with that Maybach. Having a car like that was sure to put the women back on his magic stick. It was going to be the test of time just to see if Chade could hold them off. With the love he had for Baylei, hopefully that would be enough for him not to slip down the rabbit hole.

Samir, on the other hand, was thinking about the conversation he had with Wes after he returned to the party. He thought Samir needed to reach out to Hayden about the job because it was a great opportunity for him business wise. Samir didn't have to do that though because Hayden and Lacy came to him with an offer, he couldn't refuse a couple weeks later.

The job was remote and he didn't have to go into the office unless he was needed for meetings. Hayden sent all of the electronic equipment he would need to do his daily tasks and even gave him an advance. Samir did apologize to Hayden and his wife about the misunderstanding and they accepted with no question.

Spending days going over the spreadsheet to the Vick's finances, Samir was finally at the end. So far, he hadn't come across any miscalculations. As he was tallying the end balance, his total didn't match what the bank records displayed. It was off by at least a hundred grand. Going back through the spread sheet and the receipts Hayden had provided, everything matched except six cash withdrawals. Those transactions weren't accounted for in the receipts and Samir knew he had found something. He picked up his phone and dialed Hayden.

"Samir, what you got for me?" he asked as soon as he answered.

"There are a few withdrawals that were made from last year, September through February. All of the transactions were cash withdrawals equaling a hundred thousand dollars. That's where your money is. Whoever made those withdrawals is the person that has your money. I would advise you to hit up the bank and see if there's any documentation on those transactions. They should be able to tell you who withdrew the money because for that amount, they would have needed identification and access to the account."

"Thank you for digging into this matter for me. I've already made changes to my accounts. I know who the culprit is, but I don't know where he is at the moment. To let you know, I did a thorough background check on you and I want you to take over the position as my account and financial advisor. The salary I quoted for you will increase if you agree. I'll understand if you say no. I just wanted to run it by you in case you were interest."

"Nah, I got you on whatever you need. I'm going to simplify your spreadsheets to make them easier for you to understand. You should always know what's going on with your money, with or without someone passing the information back to you."

"Don't worry about that today. Take the rest of the day off and have some fun. Get back into the dating scene, Samir. Don't waste your life waiting for Selena to decide if she's coming back or not. I love that woman like a sister, but her decisions were the wrong one to choose."

"Selena is the last person on my mind. Long as nothing happens to my daughter, I'm cool with however she chooses to live her life. It is overdue for me to have a little fun. I think I will step out for a couple hours. Send anything you need done in the email and I'll get to it first thing in the morning."

"Enjoy yourself. I don't want you doing anything other than having fun. I'll holla at you Monday." Hayden ended the call before Samir could say anything else.

Samir wanted to go out and chill. He thought about where as he headed for the shower. Samir stepped out of the steamy hot water and wrapped a towel around his waist as he stepped into his closet to choose an outfit. Deciding on a pair of black jeans and a button-down black shirt, Samir went to the kitchen and fixed himself a sandwich. It was still pretty early and he had a couple hours to spare before he would hit up the karaoke bar.

Summer had been on his mind a lot lately. They had plenty of conversations and gone on a few dates. Nothing much had come from their interactions. Summer took the friendship Samir wanted to heart and never attempted crossing the line. Samir chose the bar because he knew she went there every Thursday night. He was going to let her know he wanted more than friendship.

Being alone was for the birds. The day he saw Selena with that nigga Frank and his wife dressed to the nines like his ass was Bishop Don Juan or some damn body, he shook his head with shame. Samir couldn't believe she chose the polygamy lifestyle rather than working on her marriage. She talked all that mess about Samir cheating to end up sharing a man in the end. That was some backwards shit to him. But, if she liked it, he loved it.

Samir ate his sandwich and listened to some R&B music to pass the time. He was grooving to the music and every song was about love. Gerald Levert, Tank, Tyrese, and all the other songsters were keeping his mind on a woman that he no longer had in his life. It was time to go out and have fun with the only woman that has been there since his world was turned upside. Hopefully, this time around he'd get this relationship thing right.

Walking into the bar, the crowd was thick and everyone was having a good time. Samir looked around for Summer and didn't see her anywhere. He went to the bar and ordered a drink. The bartender asked if he wanted to run a tab and he declined immediately. He remembered the last time he was in the facility when he got tore up. That wasn't going to happen ever again.

Karaoke had started and it was hilarious because the woman on stage was howling louder than a wolf to the moon. The crowd was very disrespectful with the booing, and some even threw paper cups at her. Tears rolled down Samir's face because the patrons were ruthless in there tonight. Samir was leery about going up on stage because they would do him the same way.

"Man, they were wrong for that shit," a guy sitting next to Samir laughed. "She is going to run to the car and cry."

"They didn't have to do that to her," Samir laughed with him.

"She knew better than to go up there sounding like a cat getting its ass beat. She better go home and practice. Better yet, keep that tone in the shower."

Samir sipped his beer and kept watching the door. He decided to add his name to the list in case he decided to sing. As he walked through the crowd, he was stopped by many women, but he wasn't interested in any woman other than Summer. Being the man he was, Samir couldn't be the rude fella that dissed women. He smiled and kept it moving until he arrived at the table. Flipping through the book to look for a song selection, Samir smiled when he saw the song he wanted to sing.

Soon as he turned around, a woman grabbed his hand to dance to "Essence" by Wizkid. Samir moved to the beat as the woman winded her hips in front of him. The movement of her ass had him licking his lips as he placed his hands on her hips. They moved in sync and the crowd opened up for them to move freely. Samir was so into the dance he didn't notice Summer enter the establishment.

Wanting to see what had everybody's attention, Summer moved through the crowd and smiled. Samir was moving smoothly with the woman, and he was sexy with it too. She danced her way to them and maneuvered in between the two of them. The woman didn't want any problems so she danced to the side and kept moving to the beat by herself. Samir got into the dance once the woman he was seeking was in his presence. They tore the floor up and was all over one another. The song ended and Samir hugged her tightly before leading the way to the bar to buy Summer a drink.

"I didn't know you were coming out tonight," Summer said after placing her drink order.

"It wasn't planned. I knew you would be here, so I decided to step out."

"Awww, that was sweet of you. I've contemplated calling you to come out all week, but I didn't want to overstep my boundaries."

"What do you mean overstep your boundaries?" Samir asked.

"I don't want to pressure you to see me as more than a friend. The chemistry is there, Samir. You need to open yourself to more than friendship. I'm not rushing you, but I want to be there for you in every aspect. You have been through a lot; I know. Being married for many years and it ending the way it has for you would close anyone off to relationships and I understand that. I'm here for you whenever you need me."

The announcer called Samir's name and he rose from his seat so he could sing. Grabbing Summer by the hand, he guided her to the front of the stage and winked at her as he climbed the stairs. The crowd clapped loudly as he adjusted the mic.

"That man can sing his ass off!" someone yelled, causing everyone to laugh.

The music came on and Samir stared into Summer's eyes as he swayed back and forth with the music. The crowd got excited when they heard his song choice and there were a lot of "you better sang this song" and "he better not fuck it up" yells that made Samir step back from the mic to clear his throat.

Storming outside, rain
She keeps me home
Quiet conversation makes me warm so,

Summer rain (sweet rain)
Whispers me to sleep and wakes me up again (my rain)
Sometimes I swear I hear her call my name (I swear, I swear)
To wash the pain away
My summer rain

In the middle of the night when I'm alone
(Alone, alone, alone)
I feel her kisses on me even when she's gone
Can't wait 'til she gets home

Summer rain (yeah)
Whispers me to sleep and wakes me up again (up again)
Sometimes I swear I hear her call my name (my name, my name)
To wash the pain away
My summer rain

I don't mind if it rains forever

Let it rain, let it rain
I said I don't mind if it rains forever
Let it rain, rain, let it rain
So go ahead and make it rain.
You bring the sunshine back again
So go ahead and make it rain
Your tender touches wash away my rain...

Samir walked down the steps as he continued to sing. Standing in front of Summer, he grabbed her around the waist and brought the mic to his mouth. The crowd went wild when they realized Samir was serenading her. The reaction only made him go harder with his performance, as if he was a real entertainer.

Say, baby, would you be my summer rain
Say, baby, would you be my summer rain
Say, baby, would you be my summer rain
Say, baby, would you be, would you be my summer rain

Samir ended the song by kissing Summer fully on the lips, sealing the deal that he wanted to test the waters with her. Samir wanted to explore the possibilities of how far they could go. He would definitely do things differently with Summer. Open communication was key, and he was ready to do things right the second time around. Samir hated the fact of starting over, but he was back at one. The beginning is where everything starts. There wouldn't be an ending with Summer if he had anything to do with it.

Stay tuned for Book 4:
All For You: Sanji & Jordyn
Coming Soon

Lock Down Publications and Ca$h Presents assisted publishing packages.

BASIC PACKAGE $499
Editing
Cover Design
Formatting

UPGRADED PACKAGE $800
Typing
Editing
Cover Design
Formatting

ADVANCE PACKAGE $1,200
Typing
Editing
Cover Design
Formatting
Copyright registration
Proofreading
Upload book to Amazon

LDP SUPREME PACKAGE $1,500
Typing
Editing
Cover Design
Formatting
Copyright registration
Proofreading
Set up Amazon account
Upload book to Amazon
Advertise on LDP Amazon and Facebook page

***Other services available upon request. Additional charges may apply

Lock Down Publications
P.O. Box 944
Stockbridge, GA 30281-9998
Phone # 470 303-9761

Submission Guideline

Submit the first three chapters of your completed manuscript to ldpsubmissions@gmail.com, subject line: Your book's title. The manuscript must be in a .doc file and sent as an attachment. Document should be in Times New Roman, double spaced and in size 12 font. Also, provide your synopsis and full contact information. If sending multiple submissions, they must each be in a separate email.

Have a story but no way to send it electronically? You can still submit to LDP/Ca$h Presents. Send in the first three chapters, written or typed, of your completed manuscript to:

LDP: Submissions Dept
Po Box 944
Stockbridge, Ga 30281

DO NOT send original manuscript. Must be a duplicate.

Provide your synopsis and a cover letter containing your full contact information.

Thanks for considering LDP and Ca$h Presents.

<u>NEW RELEASES</u>

THE BIRTH OF A GANGSTER 2 by DELMONT PLAYER
LOYAL TO THE SOIL 3 by JIBRIL WILLIAMS
COKE BOYS by ROMELL TUKES
GRIMEY WAYS 2 by RAY VINCI
AN UNFORESEEN LOVE 3 by MEESHA

BLOOD OF A BOSS **VI**

SHADOWS OF THE GAME II

TRAP BASTARD II

By **Askari**

LOYAL TO THE GAME **IV**

By **T.J. & Jelissa**

TRUE SAVAGE **VIII**

MIDNIGHT CARTEL IV

DOPE BOY MAGIC IV

CITY OF KINGZ III

NIGHTMARE ON SILENT AVE II

THE PLUG OF LIL MEXICO II

CLASSIC CITY II

By **Chris Green**

BLAST FOR ME **III**

A SAVAGE DOPEBOY III

CUTTHROAT MAFIA III

DUFFLE BAG CARTEL VII

HEARTLESS GOON VI

By **Ghost**

A HUSTLER'S DECEIT III

KILL ZONE II

BAE BELONGS TO ME III

TIL DEATH II

By **Aryanna**

KING OF THE TRAP III

By **T.J. Edwards**

GORILLAZ IN THE BAY V

3X KRAZY III

STRAIGHT BEAST MODE III
De'Kari
KINGPIN KILLAZ IV
STREET KINGS III
PAID IN BLOOD III
CARTEL KILLAZ IV
DOPE GODS III
Hood Rich
SINS OF A HUSTLA II
ASAD
RICH $AVAGE II
By Martell Troublesome Bolden
YAYO V
Bred In The Game 2
S. Allen
CREAM III
THE STREETS WILL TALK II
By Yolanda Moore
SON OF A DOPE FIEND III
HEAVEN GOT A GHETTO II
By Renta
LOYALTY AIN'T PROMISED III
By Keith Williams
I'M NOTHING WITHOUT HIS LOVE II
SINS OF A THUG II
TO THE THUG I LOVED BEFORE II
IN A HUSTLER I TRUST II
By Monet Dragun
QUIET MONEY IV
EXTENDED CLIP III

THUG LIFE IV

By **Trai'Quan**

THE STREETS MADE ME IV

By **Larry D. Wright**

IF YOU CROSS ME ONCE II

ANGEL IV

By **Anthony Fields**

THE STREETS WILL NEVER CLOSE IV

By **K'ajji**

HARD AND RUTHLESS III

KILLA KOUNTY III

By **Khufu**

MONEY GAME III

By **Smoove Dolla**

JACK BOYS VS DOPE BOYS II

A GANGSTA'S QUR'AN V

COKE GIRLZ II

COKE BOYS II

By **Romell Tukes**

MURDA WAS THE CASE II

Elijah R. Freeman

THE STREETS NEVER LET GO II

By **Robert Baptiste**

AN UNFORESEEN LOVE IV

By **Meesha**

KING OF THE TRENCHES III
by **GHOST & TRANAY ADAMS**

MONEY MAFIA II

By **Jibril Williams**

QUEEN OF THE ZOO III

By **Black Migo**
VICIOUS LOYALTY III
By Kingpen
A GANGSTA'S PAIN III
By J-Blunt
CONFESSIONS OF A JACKBOY III
By Nicholas Lock
GRIMEY WAYS III
By Ray Vinci
KING KILLA II
By Vincent "Vitto" Holloway
BETRAYAL OF A THUG II
By Fre$h
THE MURDER QUEENS II
By Michael Gallon
THE BIRTH OF A GANGSTER III
By Delmont Player
TREAL LOVE II
By Le'Monica Jackson
FOR THE LOVE OF BLOOD II
By Jamel Mitchell
RAN OFF ON DA PLUG II
By Paper Boi Rari
HOOD CONSIGLIERE II
By Keese
PRETTY GIRLS DO NASTY THINGS II
By Nicole Goosby
PROTÉGÉ OF A LEGEND II
By Corey Robinson
IT'S JUST ME AND YOU II

By Ah'Million

Available Now

RESTRAINING ORDER **I & II**
By **CA$H & Coffee**
LOVE KNOWS NO BOUNDARIES **I II & III**
By **Coffee**
RAISED AS A GOON I, II, III & IV
BRED BY THE SLUMS I, II, III
BLAST FOR ME I & II
ROTTEN TO THE CORE I II III
A BRONX TALE I, II, III
DUFFLE BAG CARTEL I II III IV V VI
HEARTLESS GOON I II III IV V
A SAVAGE DOPEBOY I II
DRUG LORDS I II III
CUTTHROAT MAFIA I II
KING OF THE TRENCHES
By **Ghost**
LAY IT DOWN **I & II**
LAST OF A DYING BREED I II
BLOOD STAINS OF A SHOTTA I & II III
By **Jamaica**
LOYAL TO THE GAME I II III
LIFE OF SIN I, II III
By **TJ & Jelissa**

BLOODY COMMAS I & II

SKI MASK CARTEL I II & III

KING OF NEW YORK I II,III IV V

RISE TO POWER I II III

COKE KINGS I II III IV V

BORN HEARTLESS I II III IV

KING OF THE TRAP I II

By **T.J. Edwards**

IF LOVING HIM IS WRONG…I & II

LOVE ME EVEN WHEN IT HURTS I II III

By **Jelissa**

WHEN THE STREETS CLAP BACK I & II III

THE HEART OF A SAVAGE I II III IV

MONEY MAFIA

LOYAL TO THE SOIL I II III

By **Jibril Williams**

A DISTINGUISHED THUG STOLE MY HEART I II & III

LOVE SHOULDN'T HURT I II III IV

RENEGADE BOYS I II III IV

PAID IN KARMA I II III

SAVAGE STORMS I II III

AN UNFORESEEN LOVE I II III

By **Meesha**

A GANGSTER'S CODE I &, II III

A GANGSTER'S SYN I II III

THE SAVAGE LIFE I II III

CHAINED TO THE STREETS I II III

BLOOD ON THE MONEY I II III

A GANGSTA'S PAIN I II

By **J-Blunt**

192

PUSH IT TO THE LIMIT
By **Bre' Hayes**
BLOOD OF A BOSS **I, II, III, IV, V**
SHADOWS OF THE GAME
TRAP BASTARD
By **Askari**
THE STREETS BLEED MURDER **I, II & III**
THE HEART OF A GANGSTA I II& III
By **Jerry Jackson**
CUM FOR ME I II III IV V VI VII VIII
An **LDP Erotica Collaboration**
BRIDE OF A HUSTLA **I II & II**
THE FETTI GIRLS **I, II& III**
CORRUPTED BY A GANGSTA I, II III, IV
BLINDED BY HIS LOVE
THE PRICE YOU PAY FOR LOVE I, II ,III
DOPE GIRL MAGIC I II III
By **Destiny Skai**
WHEN A GOOD GIRL GOES BAD
By **Adrienne**
THE COST OF LOYALTY I II III
By Kweli
A GANGSTER'S REVENGE **I II III & IV**
THE BOSS MAN'S DAUGHTERS I II III IV V
A SAVAGE LOVE **I & II**
BAE BELONGS TO ME I II
A HUSTLER'S DECEIT I, II, III
WHAT BAD BITCHES DO I, II, III
SOUL OF A MONSTER I II III
KILL ZONE

A DOPE BOY'S QUEEN I II III

TIL DEATH

By **Aryanna**

A KINGPIN'S AMBITON

A KINGPIN'S AMBITION **II**

I MURDER FOR THE DOUGH

By **Ambitious**

TRUE SAVAGE I II III IV V VI VII

DOPE BOY MAGIC I, II, III

MIDNIGHT CARTEL I II III

CITY OF KINGZ I II

NIGHTMARE ON SILENT AVE

THE PLUG OF LIL MEXICO II

CLASSIC CITY

By **Chris Green**

A DOPEBOY'S PRAYER

By **Eddie "Wolf" Lee**

THE KING CARTEL **I, II & III**

By **Frank Gresham**

THESE NIGGAS AIN'T LOYAL **I, II & III**

By **Nikki Tee**

GANGSTA SHYT **I II &III**

By **CATO**

THE ULTIMATE BETRAYAL

By **Phoenix**

BOSS'N UP **I , II & III**

By **Royal Nicole**

I LOVE YOU TO DEATH

By **Destiny J**

I RIDE FOR MY HITTA

I STILL RIDE FOR MY HITTA

By **Misty Holt**

LOVE & CHASIN' PAPER

By **Qay Crockett**

TO DIE IN VAIN

SINS OF A HUSTLA

By **ASAD**

BROOKLYN HUSTLAZ

By **Boogsy Morina**

BROOKLYN ON LOCK I & II

By **Sonovia**

GANGSTA CITY

By **Teddy Duke**

A DRUG KING AND HIS DIAMOND I & II III

A DOPEMAN'S RICHES

HER MAN, MINE'S TOO I, II

CASH MONEY HO'S

THE WIFEY I USED TO BE I II

PRETTY GIRLS DO NASTY THINGS

By Nicole Goosby

TRAPHOUSE KING **I II & III**

KINGPIN KILLAZ I II III

STREET KINGS I II

PAID IN BLOOD **I II**

CARTEL KILLAZ I II III

DOPE GODS I II

By **Hood Rich**

LIPSTICK KILLAH **I, II, III**

CRIME OF PASSION I II & III

FRIEND OR FOE I II III

Meesha

By **Mimi**

STEADY MOBBN' **I, II, III**

THE STREETS STAINED MY SOUL I II III

By **Marcellus Allen**

WHO SHOT YA **I, II, III**

SON OF A DOPE FIEND I II

HEAVEN GOT A GHETTO

Renta

GORILLAZ IN THE BAY **I II III IV**

TEARS OF A GANGSTA I II

3X KRAZY I II

STRAIGHT BEAST MODE I II

DE'KARI

TRIGGADALE I II III

MURDAROBER WAS THE CASE

Elijah R. Freeman

GOD BLESS THE TRAPPERS I, II, III

THESE SCANDALOUS STREETS I, II, III

FEAR MY GANGSTA I, II, III IV, V

THESE STREETS DON'T LOVE NOBODY I, II

BURY ME A G I, II, III, IV, V

A GANGSTA'S EMPIRE I, II, III, IV

THE DOPEMAN'S BODYGAURD I II

THE REALEST KILLAZ I II III

THE LAST OF THE OGS I II III

Tranay Adams

THE STREETS ARE CALLING

Duquie Wilson

MARRIED TO A BOSS I II III

By Destiny Skai & Chris Green

KINGZ OF THE GAME I II III IV V VI
Playa Ray
SLAUGHTER GANG I II III
RUTHLESS HEART I II III
By Willie Slaughter
FUK SHYT
By Blakk Diamond
DON'T F#CK WITH MY HEART I II
By Linnea
ADDICTED TO THE DRAMA I II III
IN THE ARM OF HIS BOSS II
By Jamila
YAYO I II III IV
A SHOOTER'S AMBITION I II
BRED IN THE GAME
By S. Allen
TRAP GOD I II III
RICH $AVAGE
MONEY IN THE GRAVE I II III
By Martell Troublesome Bolden
FOREVER GANGSTA
GLOCKS ON SATIN SHEETS I II
By Adrian Dulan
TOE TAGZ I II III IV
LEVELS TO THIS SHYT I II
IT'S JUST ME AND YOU
By Ah'Million
KINGPIN DREAMS I II III
RAN OFF ON DA PLUG
By Paper Boi Rari

CONFESSIONS OF A GANGSTA I II III IV

CONFESSIONS OF A JACKBOY I II

By Nicholas Lock

I'M NOTHING WITHOUT HIS LOVE

SINS OF A THUG

TO THE THUG I LOVED BEFORE

A GANGSTA SAVED XMAS

IN A HUSTLER I TRUST

By Monet Dragun

CAUGHT UP IN THE LIFE I II III

THE STREETS NEVER LET GO

By Robert Baptiste

NEW TO THE GAME I II III

MONEY, MURDER & MEMORIES I II III

By **Malik D. Rice**

LIFE OF A SAVAGE I II III

A GANGSTA'S QUR'AN I II III IV

MURDA SEASON I II III

GANGLAND CARTEL I II III

CHI'RAQ GANGSTAS I II III

KILLERS ON ELM STREET I II III

JACK BOYZ N DA BRONX I II III

A DOPEBOY'S DREAM I II III

JACK BOYS VS DOPE BOYS

COKE GIRLZ

COKE BOYS

By Romell Tukes

LOYALTY AIN'T PROMISED I II

By Keith Williams

QUIET MONEY I II III

THUG LIFE I II III

EXTENDED CLIP I II

By **Trai'Quan**

THE STREETS MADE ME I II III

By **Larry D. Wright**

THE ULTIMATE SACRIFICE I, II, III, IV, V, VI

KHADIFI

IF YOU CROSS ME ONCE

ANGEL I II III

IN THE BLINK OF AN EYE

By **Anthony Fields**

THE LIFE OF A HOOD STAR

By Ca$h & Rashia Wilson

THE STREETS WILL NEVER CLOSE I II III

By K'ajji

CREAM I II

THE STREETS WILL TALK

By Yolanda Moore

NIGHTMARES OF A HUSTLA I II III

By King Dream

CONCRETE KILLA I II III

VICIOUS LOYALTY I II

By Kingpen

HARD AND RUTHLESS I II

MOB TOWN 251

THE BILLIONAIRE BENTLEYS I II III

By Von Diesel

GHOST MOB

Stilloan Robinson

MOB TIES I II III IV V VI

Meesha

By SayNoMore
BODYMORE MURDERLAND I II III
THE BIRTH OF A GANGSTER I II
By Delmont Player
FOR THE LOVE OF A BOSS
By C. D. Blue
MOBBED UP I II III IV
THE BRICK MAN I II III IV
THE COCAINE PRINCESS I II III IV V
By King Rio
KILLA KOUNTY I II III
By Khufu
MONEY GAME I II
By Smoove Dolla
A GANGSTA'S KARMA I II
By FLAME
KING OF THE TRENCHES I II
by **GHOST & TRANAY ADAMS**
QUEEN OF THE ZOO I II
By **Black Migo**
GRIMEY WAYS I II
By Ray Vinci
XMAS WITH AN ATL SHOOTER
By Ca$h & Destiny Skai
KING KILLA
By Vincent "Vitto" Holloway
BETRAYAL OF A THUG
By Fre$h
THE MURDER QUEENS
By Michael Gallon

200

TREAL LOVE

By Le'Monica Jackson

FOR THE LOVE OF BLOOD

By Jamel Mitchell

HOOD CONSIGLIERE

By Keese

PROTÉGÉ OF A LEGEND

By Corey Robinson

<u>BOOKS BY LDP'S CEO, CA$H</u>

TRUST IN NO MAN

TRUST IN NO MAN 2

TRUST IN NO MAN 3

BONDED BY BLOOD

SHORTY GOT A THUG

THUGS CRY

THUGS CRY 2

THUGS CRY 3

TRUST NO BITCH

TRUST NO BITCH 2

TRUST NO BITCH 3

TIL MY CASKET DROPS

RESTRAINING ORDER

RESTRAINING ORDER 2

IN LOVE WITH A CONVICT

LIFE OF A HOOD STAR

XMAS WITH AN ATL SHOOTER

Follow Me...

Facebook: https://www.facebook.com/mesha.king1
Instagram: https://www.instagram.com/author_meesha/
Twitter: https://twitter.com/AuthorMeesha
Tiktok: https://vm.tiktok.com/TTPdkx6LEW/
Website: www.authormeesha.com

CPSIA information can be obtained
at www.ICGtesting.com
Printed in the USA
LVHW081100290822
727089LV00007B/104